THE SLUM MOTHER'S SACRIFICE

VICTORIAN ROMANCE

DOLLY PRICE

PUREREAD.COM

Copyright © 2025 PureRead Ltd

www.pureread.com

All rights reserved. No part of this publication may be reproduced, distributed or transmitted in any form or by any means, without prior written permission.

Publisher's Note: This is a work of fiction. Names, characters, places, and incidents are a product of the author's imagination. Locales and public names are sometimes used for atmospheric purposes. Any resemblance to actual people, living or dead, or to businesses, companies, events, institutions, or locales is completely coincidental.

CONTENTS

Dear reader, get ready for another great story…	1
1. Poaching	3
2. Rose's Cough	13
3. The Crystal Palace	24
4. The Journey to London	35
5. Arrival in London	48
6. Letters Home	59
7. Life in the Boarding House	69
8. The Accident	79
9. Angry Words of Truth	91
10. The Investigation	103
11. An Unwelcome Admirer	115
12. A Visit to Birmingham	126
13. Complications	136
14. A Choice Must Be Made	148
15. The Heart Unveiled	160
16. A Hard Goodbye	169
17. The Bakery in Birmingham	179
18. If you loved Slum Mother's Sacrifice…	188
Love Victorian Romance?	203
Our Gift To You	205

DEAR READER, GET READY FOR ANOTHER GREAT STORY...

A VICTORIAN ROMANCE

A midst prejudice and poverty, one woman's courage will redefine what it means to be a mother.

Turn the page and let's begin

POACHING

"Let me help you with them clothes, Katie."

Katherine Foley peered around the flapping white bedsheet, although she didn't need to see who was speaking to know that Gerry Murphy was on the other side.

Gerry smiled, his warm brown eyes crinkling at the corners when his gaze met hers. Katherine smiled in return, then wished she had not done so, because Gerry's response was to smile more broadly, his visage telling her he knew that she'd mourned her dead husband a year. It was, his smile said, time to move past the dead and toward the living.

"Thank you, Gerry," she said primly, "but I'm sure you've plenty of work to do yourself and 'tis not for me to keep you from it." She batted smuts of soot from the freshly washed sheet. Too soon, it would be getting on for the cooler weather with autumn arriving. Folks who'd enjoyed the summer for its heat and the money saved in fuel would soon be burning coal and firewood. The chimneys of thousands of people in Birmingham, England, warmed the insides of tenements and palaces alike, while expelling the dust and dirt into the air.

Washing clothes for a living was hard enough for an Irish widow with two young children to raise, but it would be especially hard come winter. She'd have to hang the clothes inside the cramped two-room flat where the family lived so that the garments would dry. The rooms were crowded enough as it was: stringing a line from the front room where the cooking, eating, and washing up were done, to the tiny bedroom where she and the children slept, would make the Foleys feel even more squeezed within the walls. But it was no more than any of her neighbours, desperate Irish workers in flight from the Great Hunger who'd come to Birmingham for the sake of their families, had to deal with and in fact, the Foleys were less crowded, with only three in the dwelling.

Gerry shrugged. If he sensed a rebuff in her words, he gave no indication of it. He continued to move along the clothesline, to pluck the washed and dried linens and garments from it and put them into the waiting basket. "Where are Rose and Seamus?" he asked.

"Over at Bridey McKenna's, playing with her brood. I'll be calling them in for supper soon." Katherine folded the shirt as neatly as she could, so that ironing it would be easier.

"Supper," Gerry said as he removed another sheet from the clothesline. "I'm still dreaming of that grand stew you made not a month ago."

He smiled when he said it to take the edge off his bald effort to invite himself to the family meal. Gerry was a charming man, and good looking, with the brown beard and moustache that he found time to keep neat and trim despite his long hours at the textile mill. He was hard-working and kind, patient and attentive with children, traits no doubt earned as the eldest of a raucous brood of siblings. He didn't drink more than the average and didn't spend his wages in the taverns. He laughed easily and went to mass on Sundays. If she were looking for a husband to replace Jimmy, Gerry would have been the obvious choice.

He certainly thought so. But Katherine wasn't looking. Jimmy Foley, big and brawny, with a laugh as vivid and loud as his carrot-red hair, had gone to his death on the public works back home in Ballygowl.

"Speaking of that fine stew," Gerry said, lowering his voice, "I'm thinking it's time for another. What d'you say?"

Katherine maintained a noncommittal expression as she took down another garment from the line. Inside, however, her heart started racing with the combination of eagerness and fear that always greeted an announcement that Gerry was ready to go poaching again.

It would mean a night of no rest in order to leave the teeming noise and eyes of Birmingham to walk to the farthest outskirts of the city, far enough that the dense, dark woods replaced the sleepless, watchful eyes of the slums. It meant being vigilant and awake through the night to quickly snare a pair of rabbits or partridges that could be surreptitiously killed and hidden in a satchel to be brought back home for skinning and gutting. And cooking, for poaching meant meat for her children, a welcome reprieve from the gruel, potato parings, and rotting vegetables that made up their daily fare. Another stew, strengthened by meat and perhaps a few fresh vegetables if she could spare the money for them, would do wonders for Rose and Seamus, especially now with Rose so prone to coughs. Katherine could use the bones to make broth, which would add flavour to a soup, even if the vegetables she'd be able to afford would be past their best days.

Katherine hid her face from view as she lowered her head to fold the man's shirt she'd taken off the line and put it into the basket. If her mother were alive now, she'd be mortified to think that her daughter had turned to poaching to feed her family. But Ma had died before the Famine, and Pa had died before her. They'd known hunger, but not starvation.

"Aye," she said, not meeting Gerry's intent gaze as she brushed a loose lock of damp auburn hair that had come loose from the pins. "When?"

"I'm thinking night after next," Gerry said. "Should be a clear night, Ma says her bones tell her it's not going to rain." He grinned, accepting his mother's rheumatism as sufficient proof of the weather forecast. "A clear night, a three-quarter moon . . ."

"Do you not think we ought to wait," Katherine said anxiously, "for an overcast night when we're less likely to be seen?"

"And risk the rain?" Gerry scoffed. "We'd get naught but mud and chills for our efforts."

Katherine knew he was right. Gerry had been working and living in Birmingham for two years, providing for his family with the wages he earned from the textile mill and from a spot of poaching now and again. He had four sisters and a brother whose ages ranged from eleven to sixteen, and a mother who took care of their lodgings and did the cooking and cleaning. Mary Murphy seemed to have no qualms about her son's illegal means of procuring food for the family, but then, Mary was a fierce Irish patriot who regarded the poaching of English game as one way of striking back at the loathed tyrants. Katherine's mother although not fond of the English, had been even less fond of lawbreaking.

Seeing her hesitate, Gerry said, coaxingly, "Ah, c'mon now, lass, 'tis food for your children and the forest has plenty more. 'Tisn't as though we're trespassing on some great lord's property now."

Katherine knew that Gerry was trying to make her feel better by smoothing the rough edges of laws which, in his view, were designed to keep the poor downtrodden.

Although Gerry didn't discuss politics with her, Katherine knew that he and his mother, indeed, the entire Murphy family, were passionate Fenians, dedicated, at least in their speech, to ridding Ireland of the cursed invaders who had robbed the Irish of their liberty long before a potato was ever planted in an Irish field. For the Murphys and their forebears, and many of the other Irish who lived in the Birmingham slums, worked in Birmingham factories, and starved on Birmingham wages, the resentments against the English had not abated since Henry the Second and his Normans invaded the island in the twelfth century.

Jimmy had always stayed out of politics. It was his dream that someday the Irish would be led by canny politicians who would guide the nation to independence, but he didn't favour violence as a means. *O Jimmy*, Katherine thought as she weighed the limited options before her, *I do miss your good sense.*

But Jimmy wouldn't want his children to go hungry.

Katherine nodded, saying nothing. There was no need to voice her assent. Poaching was serious business, with a severe punishment. She could be transported from England to the wilds of Australia, and then what would happen to her children?

"Aye, then," Gerry commented, reading her acquiescence. "Saturday, then. I'll send Althne over to your crib to mind Rose and Seamus. She'll keep her wits about her."

Althne was the eldest of the sisters, a quiet, responsible girl who could be trusted to see to the children. She would, of course, know where her brother and Katherine were going but she'd never let on to the children or to anyone.

"Thank you," Katherine said. She might have been thanking Gerry for picking up the basket of folded laundry and carrying it into her lodgings, but they both knew that there was a greater reason for her appreciation. By including her in his forays to the forest to poach, Gerry was helping her to provide for her family. Katherine knew that he was a good-hearted young man, genuinely fond of the children and willing to help a widow if he could. She also knew that the day would come when Gerry would naturally assume that his kindly gestures would be accepted as wooing, and that, when she thought herself ready, he would be the man she'd choose to be a father to Rose and Seamus. She could not think of such a development now, so she thanked him again.

He paused at the door, his brown eyes resting upon her

face as if he found it pleasant to do so. "If you need aught," he said, "you know where to find me."

"Two streets down, first door in," she repeated. It was how Gerry had introduced himself when she'd first moved into her two-room lodging, in Birmingham. She'd sold nearly everything they had owned to pay for the journey to Birmingham and the flat, with its uneven floor, smoke-stained ceiling, and windows papered over to keep out the draft where the glass had cracked, was all she could afford. She could have cried when the children looked around in mute disbelief.

It had been Gerry who'd found furniture for her to use: a table, wobbly to be sure, but it worked for them; a bench to sit on made of a rough-hewn plank with no shortage of splinters; a straw tick mattress big enough for the three of them to sleep on; an odd mismatch of plates and cups; threadbare blankets that kept them covered if not entirely warm in chilly weather; and various items that she was grateful to receive.

He'd found her customers so that she could earn wages doing laundry and he'd brought her a big metal tub and a washboard, crowing with triumph because he'd bargained successfully for it. He'd refused to take so much as a shilling for anything, claiming that the Irish had to stick together or the accursed English would rob them blind. Then he'd apologized, with a cheery smile, for bringing the English into what was meant to be a civil conversation.

Gerry grinned. "Never forget it," he said. "Now, lock the door after me. There's ruffians about."

He always cautioned her against being lax in keeping her home secure. She knew the streets were not safe, for even though there were many fellow Irish living as her neighbours, there were just as many thieves, drunkards, and ne-er-do-wells. Not a night went by, after she and the children had said their prayers and Rose and Seamus were sleeping soundly, one on each side of her, that Katherine didn't lie awake and long for the familiarity of the green fields of home, where she had never locked her door nor had reason to.

"Saturday night, then," he said softly as he stood outside the door to leave.

"Saturday night," she whispered, closing the door.

As Katherine added water to stretch the precious cooking oil in the frying pan, she stood over the fire, stirring in the potato peels and the cabbage she'd gotten from the street vendor that morning, and tried to stave off the rising momentum of fears. How much longer could she live like this? The children were growing out of their clothing—how would she afford the thread, the cloth, everything she'd need to sew them something new? When cold came, how would she afford the extra wood she'd need to keep the fire going so that the laundry would dry inside the kitchen? What if Rose suffered another cough like the one she'd had last winter? What would Katherine do for medicine?

The walls of the rooms in which she and the children lived felt as if they were pressing closer, as if they intended to trap her inside this dismal place so that she would never again wake up to the sun on her face in the morning and the lush, verdant countryside all around her. If she did not find some way of protecting her children from the poverty and despair which engulfed Birmingham as much as the thick shroud of smoke from the coal fires that kept the factories running, she would never be able to make Jimmy's dreams for his son and daughter come true.

ROSE'S COUGH

The blood stains in the handkerchiefs had faded to pink from Katherine's rigorous scrubbing. Katherine's heart was heavy as she took the squares of cloth down from the cord she'd strung across the width of the main room. Outside, the night noise maintained its raucous chorus of revellers and prostitutes and thieves taking advantage of the darkness. But Katherine's ears were attuned to the sounds of her children asleep on the mattress in the tiny alcove that served as their bedroom. Rose had had a bad day of it, with the coughing that left bloody marks on the handkerchiefs. She seemed to be sleeping peacefully now; perhaps the pectoral balsam of honey that Katherine had obtained from the chemist was doing her daughter some benefit.

Katherine had sold her bonnet so that she would have the money for the medicine, and even though the chemist had scowled at her request, he'd filled a bottle for her, warning her that the mixture contained opium and ought to only be dispensed in great moderation.

Katherine sat down on the stool in front of the fire and began folding the clothes she'd taken down from the line. Folding clothes afforded her too much time to think. It was then that she addressed her diminishing funds. After she paid the next week's rent, they would not have enough money for food, never mind medicine for Rose. Katherine's mind went over the inventory of her belongings: what could she sell? Nothing that belonged to the children. Jimmy Foley's offspring, Seamus already dressed like beggars in too-short trousers and Rose with too-tight sleeves, had nothing to spare. Katherine had sold her best dress and now attended mass on Sundays wearing the same frock she used when she washed clothes, swept the fireplace, and skinned the rabbits that she and Gerry poached on rare occasions.

What was she to do? The only option that was open to a woman in the slums of Birmingham when she had nothing left to sell was to offer herself at a price. That Katherine would not do. Jimmy Foley's widow would not turn to whoring.

But she could not let her children starve, nor let Rose die of the consumption that Katherine was sure was her daughter's lung complaint.

The next morning, Rose was groggy when Katherine roused her from sleep. Seamus looked at his younger sister with a mixture of brotherly affection and alarm. "Wake up, lazybones," he teased as Rose's eyelids fluttered but didn't open.

Katherine patted her daughter's cheek, lightly tapping the skin so that Rose would stir into wakefulness. She bit her lip in fear. The pectoral balsam of honey, with its opiate included in the ingredients, might have been too much for the child's system to handle.

"Ma," Seamus said, "why don't you put a cold cloth on her face? That'll rouse her."

Katherine nodded eagerly at her son's resourcefulness. "You go fetch the water, won't you?"

Seamus put on his cap and raced out the door without his coat. But fortunately, the winter was gone and spring, with its delicate promise of warmer days, was underway.

Even as she held her daughter in her arms and crooned one of her own mother's favourite songs, Katherine's brain was in a frenzy tallying up what she'd save when she didn't need to buy as much wood to keep warm.

Perhaps when the warm weather came to stay, there would be a few pennies here and there that could be saved up for Rose to get proper care for her lungs. Perhaps she'd be able to take in more laundry. Perhaps she'd save a bit and sew new clothes for the children, or else buy used clothing from one of the many vendors plying their trade up and down the streets of the Birmingham slum. Perhaps she'd save enough money so that they could go back to Ireland—

Perhaps, perhaps, always perhaps. Nothing but hope, and that hope a desolate one.

She confided her fears to Gerry when he stopped by later in the evening with three onions he'd bought off a greengrocer on his way home from his new job at the glass factory.

"For an onion poultice," he explained to Katherine's puzzled glance. "For Rosie."

Tears flooded Katherine's eyes at Gerry's kindness. He patted her awkwardly. "Ma swears by 'em and when I told her how Rosie's coughing so, she reminded me of what she always did for us when we were ailing. Where is Rosie now?"

"She's gone back to sleep," Katherine told him. "She was up for a while, but the pectoral balsam of honey. . ," the tears came again, faster. "I should never have given it to her. The chemist told me it has opium but I thought it would just be enough to ease her coughing so she could sleep. She's been sluggish all day. I'm so afraid, Gerry—"

Katherine didn't know how it happened, but she found herself leaning against Gerry's shoulder, sobbing. He wrapped his arm around her, murmuring familiar soothing Gaelic words that her mother had used when she was a child.

She forced herself to move away from the comfort he offered and wIped her weeping eyes with a corner of her apron.

"So, then," she said with deliberate cheerfulness she was far from feeling. "Enough of my tears. How's the new job then? Do you like it?"

Gerry recognized the change in subject for what it was as Katherine sat apart from him. They were seated side by side on the stoop outside Katherine's rooms. Seamus had gone off to play with some of the other boys in their neighbourhood. Rose slept inside while Katherine sat outside with the door partway open so that she could hear her daughter if she began coughing.

"Eh," Gerry said, his eyes crinkling, "you do know what they call us here in Birmingham, the city of one thousand trades. The World's workshop. Working in the glass factory, it's got better pay and hours than the textile mill. It's not paradise, though."

Katherine sensed that Gerry was being deliberately vague on the drawbacks of his new occupation. She'd heard that the labourers in the glass factories worked in dangerous conditions and that the heat was almost unbearable. Still . . .

"I've been wondering if I ought to give up washing clothes and find something that pays better, like what the girls make in the mills. But I can't bear the thought of not being with Rose and Seamus. Being gone all day and leaving them on their own . . ." it's not what I'd choose." She was going to say that it wasn't what Jimmy Foley would have wanted, but she refrained. Gerry had brought her onions for a poultice for Rose's chest and while she knew that his generosity was genuine, she understood that he had a different price in mind.

Gerry shook his head and took her hand briefly, then released it, mindful that they were not alone. Katherine had her pride and she'd be smarting now for sure at having let herself give into her tears in public view. "You're where you ought to be. The children, they need you. I'll keep my eyes open. Maybe something will come up."

Gerry continued to stop by at least once a week to ask about Rose and Seamus. The onion poultices helped but they did not stop the coughing that the little girl suffered. A night's poaching in the forest brought meat for meals so that Katherine could feed the children heartier fare for a brief time. But when she and Gerry were nearly caught by the constable as they left the forest on a moonlit night with the rabbits in the satchel, and saved themselves only because the constable was fat and they were much faster, she vowed that she would never put herself at risk in such a way.

Gerry understood her concerns. She was all that her children had. He promised that he'd be on the watch for something that would suit her, that paid more so that she could send Rose to a sanitorium for proper medical care, and provide money so that Seamus could go to the school run by Father Cleary of Our Lady of Sorrows parish.

Summer brought with it the more temperate weather that required less firewood. With the savings she garnered by spending less, Katherine bought a discarded bolt of cloth that had been in a shop window and was faded by the sunlight. She sewed Seamus a new shirt and for Rose, a new dress. The children were so delighted with the garments that it nearly brought Katherine to tears.

One summer evening in July, she was siting by the window, sewing buttons onto the

shirts she'd washed, a task which brought in a bit of extra money, when she spied Gerry walking up the street with a purposeful gait. She put down the shirt and her needle and went to the door to open it before he knocked. Rose was sleeping, worn out by a day's coughing, and Katherine didn't want her to be awakened by their voices.

Gerry looked jubilant. "Didn't I tell you I'd keep me eyes open for something for you?" he said happily as he sat down on the stoop.

'You've found something?" Katherine asked him, spreading the skirt of her dress as she sat down beside him.

"You'll never believe it. There's an engineer, name of Paxton, who came by the factory this week. He's ordered glass, lots of it, for the Crystal Palace they're building in London."

Katherine had heard of the Crystal Palace. It was a fancy of Prince Albert, husband to the Queen, to host an international gathering of inventors who would show off their creations under one roof. The Crystal Palace would be made of glass. That fact alone seemed peculiar to Katherine, who was too occupied with her own concerns to bother with the goings-on down in London. She couldn't see how anything about the Crystal Palace could affect her. She wasn't even sure what it was that an engineer did.

"Sixty thousand panes of glass," Gerry went on admiringly. "It's sure to be grand."

Katherine let Gerry talk. The evening air felt good on her skin. She'd finished up seven loads of laundry which she'd deliver tomorrow. There would be an extra shilling or two from the mending she'd done. She could buy more onions to make poultices for Rose, and maybe something to tempt the child's diminished appetite.

"---And he's looking for workers. Lots of workers. I thought of you right off."

The enthusiasm in Gerry's voice jolted Katherine from her thoughts. "Workers?" she repeated blankly.

Gerry laughed. "Aye, workers. The work is scheduled to start in August so there's not much time. It's a rare tight schedule they're running on if the Great Exhibition is to open on time in May next year. I'd go if I could, but I can't leave Ma and the weans. The older girls are working, but Finola is walking out with James Ryan's lad, so she's saving all she can for them to marry with."

Katherine nodded. She knew that with Althne now in the convent, Finola was the other wage-earner in the Murphy family. They depended upon Gerry more than ever, not simply for his wages but for the efficient manner in which he managed his boisterous family.

She stared at Gerry with confusion, "London," she repeated as if she must have heard him wrong. "You're thinking of me going to London? What about Rose and Seamus?"

Gerry didn't shift from where he was sitting, but he leaned closer, his upper body taking up the space between them. "They can stay with us Murphys," he said as if the answer were obvious. "You know they'll be looked after.

Ma doesn't miss mass and she'll take them with her, just like she does the rest. I'll be there to make sure they mind the priest and don't get into mischief. Ma can go on teaching Rose her letters like you've been doing. They'll be fed and there's room now, with Finola leaving to marry soon, and Althne with the Sisters of Mercy."

"But—you want me to leave my children? Katherine's expression revealed her consternation. Her children! Everything she did was for them, every thought, waking or sleeping, was of them. "Who'll tend to Rose?" she demanded.

"Katie," Gerry said quietly, 'you know Rose is ill. She needs medical care, not onion poultices."

"They help," Katherine insisted, her lips trembling at what seemed an accusation. "I'm doing all I can for her!"

"Aye Katie, you are, but with the wages you bring in doing laundry, you can't afford what she needs. A sanitorium."

He'd said it! He'd uttered the word that Katherine could not allow herself to speak. By doing so, he also identified the true nature of what ailed Rose. Katherine began to cry, quiet, furtive tears that would not rouse her daughter from her needed sleep. She put her hand to her head in silent grief, overwhelmed by the reality of what she would need to do in order to care for her family.

"Katie," Gerry went on, "it's no more than plenty of others are doing. London's where you can earn more. Enough to pay for Rose to get care, enough to send back so that Seamus has what he needs. You trust me, don't you? You're not thinking that I'd be off to the pub, buying poteen instead of seeing that Seamus and Rose both got the food and clothing they need?"

That was not her worry. Gerry was honest and kind. He genuinely cared for her children and he looked after his own family as if he were their father, having accepted the responsibilities that went with being the eldest son and breadwinner. It was not apprehension for how her children would be treated if she left them in the Murphys' care. It was how she could respect herself if she left her children. And, that nagging reminder in the back of her thoughts, where she kept the private concerns that she trusted the Blessed Virgin to discern and understand, that Gerry would have a right to expect more from her later for what he offered now. No one expected her to remain a widow for the rest of her life.

THE CRYSTAL PALACE

Katherine gnawed on her lower lip as she waited in what seemed to be an endless line of people who looked as hard-up as she was, waiting for their turn to write their names on the list. She recognized many of the faces of the others who wanted to sign up to work on the Crystal Palace. Some of the younger faces bore expressions of eagerness at the prospect of going to London to work on the enterprise that offered not only an opportunity for employment, but what seemed a chance to be part of something magnificent, more magnificent than weaving textiles or making matches.

But the others, the ones who, like Katherine, were going not because they sought excitement but because they needed to provide for their families, bore haunted expressions. Their eyes watched the movement of the line with a mixture of impatience and dread. They were in a hurry to get this underway and reluctant to commit to it.

A bearded gentleman with a fine suit walked up and down the line, nodding with approval at the queue, rubbing his gloved hands together as if he were eager to get to work.

"That's 'im," whispered someone in line behind her. "That's Paxton. Started out as a farmer's son, caught the notice of the Duke of Devonshire. Now he's a Member of Parlyment, no less, and running this 'ere Great Exhibition."

Several people ahead of Katherine turned around to better hear what was being said. There was little enough known about the work they would be employed to do and therefore any morsel of information was seized upon as clarification.

To Katherine's surprise, she spotted Peter Edgewood looking back. Why, she wondered, was Peter leaving Birmingham? His father was a baker in the city; the aroma of the loaves of bread that were baking early in the morning wafted over the neighbourhood every day but Sunday, combatting the noxious odours of industry that hung heavily in the air as the hours progressed. Peter had an Irish mother, Maeve, who worked with her husband in the bakery. Peter worked there as well. Why would he leave?

Peter, noticing her attention, gave her a friendly but fleeting smile. Katherine was embarrassed to be caught looking at him. He was, admittedly, a fine-looking man, tall and broad-shouldered, with a riot of brown curls that always seemed to be in motion whether from his own movement or from the breezes passing through, and acute blue eyes. Just now, the blue eyes looked bleak and his shoulders were slumped forward beneath his jacket.

If he didn't want to go, Katherine wondered, then why was he in line? A bakery was a solid business, surely; people always needed bread, and sure, they wanted the pies and tarts that were for sale as well.

Her curiosity took over, her troubled thoughts, only for the moment.

The line had moved in the meantime. She saw Peter's tall frame lean over the wooden table where Mr. Paxton's secretary sat, an inkwell before him and a pen in hand that he extended to each new person in line.

The secretary was nodding. "The train leaves in one week," he said, his mutton-chop whispers concealing most of his mouth so that his words might have been coming forth from ginger-coloured fur. "Be at the train station at five of the clock sharp. If you're not on time, we won't wait. Understand?"

She saw Peter nod respectfully. "Yes, I understand," he answered in the lyrical mix of accents that came of having a Birmingham father and a Dublin mother. "I'll be there at five, sharp."

Two more people ahead of her. She forgot about Peter, her eyes anxiously awaiting her turn. One more person ahead. Then—

The secretary's eyes narrowed. "You can make your sign," he said brusquely. "On the line there."

Katherine was affronted by his assumption that she could not write.

"I'll write my name, sir, if you please," she answered with a trace of hauteur. Irish she might be, and poor as well, but she knew how to read and write.

The secretary studied her, his eyes not unkind as he did so.

What did he see? Katherine wondered. Did he see a tired woman who looked like she needed to sleep if she was going to be able to do the work she was signing up for? Did he see the patched green shawl and the shabby brown dress and think dismissively that she was yet another Irish peasant fleeing the failed potatoes that had spurred so many of her countrymen to leave? Or did he note that she'd taken special pains to fashion her auburn hair in an orderly bun at the base of her neck, with pins in place, and that she'd washed up carefully so that none of the city soot marked her as a resident of the slums? His expression gave away nothing.

He handed the pen to her.

"Sign your name, then, and your residence."

She took the pen and wrote, in her best hand, the information he required.

To her surprise, when she handed the pen back to him, he turned the book around to read what she'd written.

"Katherine Foley," he read. He turned the book around again "You write a fair hand. You're the first woman yet who's known how to write her name."

His conversation had drawn the attention of Sir Joseph Paxton, who came over to the table to see why the line had slowed down.

The secretary held up the book so that Paxton could read it.

"A fair hand, sir," he repeated.

Paxton scrutinized Katherine. "Yes," he said, answering his secretary but looking at her.

Behind her, Katherine could hear feet stamping, people shifting, impatient for their

turn and irked that there was a delay.

"There's plenty of work to do at the Crystal Palace," Paxton said.

"I'm happy to help where I am needed," Katherine replied.

"Yes, glad to hear it. Tell me . . . you're Irish, aren't you?"

Katherine stiffened, readying herself for an insult or a rebuke. "I am, sir," she declared proudly.

"Beautiful land, Ireland," Paxton said. "The greenest country I've ever seen. Do you garden at all, Mrs—" he leaned back to read her name. "Mrs Foley?"

"I did in Ireland, sir," she told him truthfully. "There's little opportunity for it here."

"Yes," he agreed, looking around him at the mass of buildings built so close together that there were spaces with no grass at all. "It's a pity, really. My Crystal Palace will celebrate British industry, but the building will be a greenhouse in its construction. I intend to have plants and flowers to adorn the structure. It's a new sort of emporium I have in mind. Nothing has ever been done to match it."

Now the people behind her were grumbling. She could hear them, in accents representing the British tongue as it was spoken from northern England, from Scotland, Wales, and of course, Ireland. Katherine could feel annoyed gazes boring holes into her back.

She wanted to get out of this line and get on her way. She had signed. What more was required?

"I was a gardener once," Paxton said, sounding almost wistful at the memory. "There's nothing like the pleasure of bringing forth God's flowers from the dirt. It's rather like recreating the Garden of Eden."

Katherine answered before thinking. "It is so in Ireland, sir. St. Patrick, he drove out the snakes. The world would have followed a different path if he'd been there."

Paxton broke out in a peal of laughter, and even the secretary managed a faint smile.

"Perhaps so," Paxton agreed. "Mrs Foley, we shall put your Irish botanical skills to good use in the Crystal Palace."

He commenced to walking down the line again, perhaps envisioning the people at work upon his Crystal Palace.

"Be at the train station at five of the clock sharp. If you're not on time, we won't wait. Understand?" The secretary repeated the instructions he had given to Peter.

She nodded. "I understand."

Katherine was glad to step out of the line. She had signed. The deed was done. It was not what Jimmy Foley would have wanted, the mother of his children leaving them with another family to go off and work in London.

"Oh, Jimmy," she thought, pained at the realization of what a turn their lives had made since Jimmy had died. "If only you'd lived. If you were still with us, I'd not be leaving Rose and Seamus, and we'd be together. We'd still be in Ireland."

But when Gerry stopped by that evening after work, she put on a brave face.

"The train leaves in a week," she said, after she'd relayed the details of meeting Mr. Paxton and his comments. "It's not much time. I have so much to do."

Gerry took her hand. It didn't matter that they were on the front step of her rooms and that all the neighbourhood was out and about, enjoying the balmy summer day. Katherine understood the underlying meaning of his action. She would be leaving her children with his family. That said as much as the banns being announced in church or a ring on her finger. Her children would be living with the Murphys. One day, they would be Murphys.

There was nothing she could do about that. She had accepted the consequences the moment that she realized her first duty was to her children. Rose needed medical care and the money for a doctor was not going to be found in Birmingham.

"We have a lot to discuss," Gerry said. His eyes were intent upon her face. Katherine recognized the look. It was a husband's look, or at least, the look of a man who recognized the woman who was destined to be his wife. She had seen the look on Jimmy's face and when she was just out of her girlhood. She still thought of herself as Jimmy Foley's wife, even if the neighbourhood saw her as a young widow who would one day remarry.

"Yes, I want to discuss Rose and Seamus with you," Katherine dodged. "They're very good children and well-behaved, but there may be some moments of impudence. They've never been out of my care. I'll make it clear to them that they owe you and your mother the respect they would give to me. Of course, I expect them to write to me once a week. Rose will need help with her spelling, but Seamus will manage well, I think, although he may fuss over having to write every week," she smiled indulgently. "I shall write to them. I'm wondering how to send money back to you for Rose's care and of course to cover the expenses of my children."

"That isn't what I meant, Katie," Gerry protested, his countenance showing a glimpse of frustration.

Katherine could not endure a conversation about romantic entanglements now when she had to fortify herself for the prospect of leaving her children behind while she went to an unknown city—London, of all places—to work. "I know," she said kindly, placing her hand upon his wrist. "You and your mother are being most generous in taking on the care of two children, but it's very important to me that we establish the—the responsibilities that go with it."

She didn't want to hurt Gerry. Nor did she want to encourage him. "I'll be in a better state of mind," she went on, somewhat evasively, "when I'm back here, and the work is finished, and I've made a bit of money, I'll have my thoughts set on the future. When Rose is better."

It was an oblique response, not at all what Gerry wanted to hear, but it was not a rejection of his attentions. Nor was it dishonest. Perhaps, in time, she would regard remarriage in a different light. Certainly, if that were so, she would want an Irishman, a Catholic, a man who didn't spend his free time in the shebeen with a bottle held to his lips and his wages going out to the barkeeper. He would need to work and save and be a father to her children.

Gerry looked away for a moment. The children, Seamus among them, were playing a game which involved running from one sidewalk to the opposite, laughing and running as they avoided the horse droppings and leavings of the emptied slop jars in the street.

"You know how I feel, Katherine," he said. "I only want you to think of me." He tried to laugh. "I don't want you falling for one of those London toffs."

It was easy to laugh at such a thought. "Hard enough it will be to spend my days surrounded by the English," she assured him.

"Oh, you'll have plenty of folk from home working with you," Gerry assured her. "If I hadn't to look after Ma and the family, sure I'd be there with you."

"Oh, that reminds me. You'll never guess who else is going to work at the Crystal Palace," Katherine said, deftly bringing the conversation to an innocuous detour. "Peter Edgewood, the baker's son. I can't fathom why a baker would want to leave for London."

As she'd hoped, Gerry was redirected. "Word is that when Aloysius Edgewood bought those new ovens, he couldn't afford to make the payments without raising prices on his goods. Folks grumbled, but paid. Well, next thing you know, the landlord hears of it and he, reckoning that Edgewood must be turning a fair profit, ups and raises his rent. If Peter is going to London, it's not for a lark. He's likely planning to send home money as well to help out his folks."

That made sense to Katherine, Why would anyone leave his family and go to London unless he, like she, was desperate?

THE JOURNEY TO LONDON

Katherine had packed her carpetbag earlier in the day. She'd put out a traveling dress that Althne, who wore a habit in the convent, had given to her to wear for the train trip from Birmingham to London. Her shoes were polished. She'd bathed and washed her hair. She was ready for the morning.

This night belonged to her children. Gerry had invited the family over to the Murphy's rooms for a send-off, but he'd understood when Katherine explained that she needed to spend this last night with Rose and Seamus. She would bring the children to the Murphy home early in the morning, and then Gerry would walk her to the train station.

The children didn't understand why she had to leave, even when she explained that she'd be making more money during the building of the Crystal Palace. She tried to make it sound as though this would be a great adventure when in truth, she could barely stand to think of parting from them.

"You'll be grand at the Murphys," she assured them as the three of them sat over supper. Katherine had splurged, getting a slice of ham from the butcher that morning, and frying it with potatoes and onions. She'd also bought a seed cake, several days old and not quite fresh, but still good, Peter assured her when he wrapped it for her.

Peter hadn't looked any more enthusiastic about the forthcoming journey than she was, and there was some comfort in knowing that she was not alone in her private sorrow. "Mrs Murphy makes the best soda bread, doesn't she? And Gerry, he's like a big brother to you."

"But you won't be there, mam," Rose replied tearfully.

Katherine bit her lip to prevent herself from crying. "Not now, I won't, but I'm coming back, pet," Katherine assured her. "It's just so that I can make more money. You'll be seeing a doctor so that you won't cough so much. Seamus, you'll be getting lessons. I spoke to Father Cleary last Sunday and he's agreed to teach you."

Neither child was enamoured of the opportunities which Katherine tried to present as something which would ease the separation.

"I don't want to go," Katherine admitted. "I didn't want to

come to Birmingham after your father died, but we had no choice. It hasn't turned out badly, has it?"

The children had adjusted to their new life in the crowded, bustling industrial metropolis. Moving away from Ireland had, in some ways, made the loss of their father easier to bear because they weren't at home to miss him.

However, she had not reckoned on her children's logic.

"Da didn't come with us when we moved," Seamus pointed out rationally, his russet locks tousled and his eyes, Jimmy's blue eyes, sombre.

"Your father is with the angels in heaven," Katherine said, keeping her voice level. She poured more tea into their cups. "Eat and drink, and when I come home, we'll have a grand feast, I promise."

"What if God takes you to be with the angels?" Rose asked tremulously, her eyes, blue like her brother's and her father's, filling with tears.

A kick to the shins would have been easier to bear. Katherine leaned over the table and wiped away the tears that had begun to fall from her daughter's gaunt cheeks. She brushed away the loose strands of red-gold hair that would likely darken to auburn as she grew older, as Katherine's had done. "Why, Rose Foley!" she declared. "Why should that happen? I'm fit and well and I'm going to London to make money for our family. I'll be much too busy to go off with the angels!"

She forced gaiety into her voice, forcing a smile to her lips as she assured the children that the angels would not be taking her anywhere. "They'll be with me, to be sure, and they'll be with you, because we're apart, and the angels know that we're going to miss each other. That is why," she began, warming to her selected topic and navigating it away from their fears, "you need to send me a letter every week."

"But mam," Rose protested, "I don't know enough words."

"Oh, my blessing," Katherine said, reaching across the table to scoop her daughter onto her lap, "If all you write is 'I love you, mam' every week, it will be enough for me."

"Is that all I have to write?" Seamus inquired hopefully.

Katherine crooked her finger and Seamus left his seat and went to her. She gathered him onto her lap, holding her two children close. "Oh, no, me lad, you'll need to write me four lines a week. I want to know what you're doing and what you're learning.

Gerry will tell me if you're minding him, so don't be thinking that just because I'm in London that I won't know what you scamps are up to. I've got me spies, you know," she warned them in just that way that Jimmy used to do, his eyes alight with merriment.

The children giggled, both of them, until Rose began to cough. Katherine held Rose close to her breast and closed her eyes. "I'll have the money to send you for the care you'll need, darling, Rosie," she told her daughter, giving her the nickname Jimmy had given her. "Let's say a prayer, shall we? I want you to pray every night. The Blessed Mother will hear you, for she is a mother too." Katherine's arms spread across her children's bodies, treasuring their closeness and storing this moment as a memory for the separation to come. "Mary, Mother of God," she began. "Hold Rose and Seamus in Thy care while we are apart. May they feel my love through Thee, so that they know we are always together, even if we are separated. Thou knowest what good children they are, Blessed Mother. Look after them and keep them safe in Thy tender care."

"And, Blessed Mother," piped up Rose, "Take care of our mam and bring her back to us."

"Bring her back," Seamus echoed. He gripped her hand with his. "Don't let the angels take her like they took our Da."

Gerry was waiting at her door the next morning. Without a word, he picked Seamus up in his arm, and took Katherine's carpetbag from her hand. Katherine was holding her sleeping daughter. They walked in silence to the Murphy lodgings.

It was still dark, but dawn would break soon. Workers were already heading off to the mills, moving like outlined shadows in the early hour. Katherine was relieved that the children were too sleepy to react to her leave-taking. She thought for certain that if either child wept, she would not be able to leave them and she'd forego the employment that was her only hope of providing the means for Rose to be treated for her lung ailment.

Mrs Murphy was outside her lodgings, waiting for them. She took Rose from Katherine's arms. "I'll put her in bed and let her sleep," she promised in a whisper. "I'll write you."

Katherine nodded, not trusting herself to speak. She followed forlornly into the rooms. The younger children were still asleep and the rooms were quiet, although a single candle on the table provided light in the kitchen, where the tea kettle was already steaming over the fireplace.

Gerry and Mrs Murphy took the children into the bedroom where the children slept. Katherine didn't follow. She felt tears beginning to rise within her, and with the tears, the painful wrenching ache of loving them so much that there was only hurt now at leaving them.

Gerry emerged and took her arm. "They're still asleep," he assured her. "They'll be well. I'll treat them as if they were my own."

He squeezed her hand. Katherine was so relieved by his promise that she squeezed his hand in response. "Gerry, I'm ever so grateful to you and your mother for this."

"Shhhh," he said, wiping her cheeks where tears had trickled down past her cheeks. "You'll be fine and so will they. I'll talk to Father Cleary about treatment for Rose."

"I spoke to him after mass on Sunday. As soon as I get my wages, I'll see to it that money is sent."

They began walking toward the train station. Katherine's feet felt too heavy to move froward. With every step, she felt the weight of her decision burdening her as if she were carrying her children in her arms all this way. It was for them that she had made the decision to go to London, but what comfort was that now, when the departure day was here and no way of knowing when she would be able to leave London and come home to resume her life in Birmingham again?

"I'll be sending the money to you every payday," she promised. "I don't know when we'll get our wages, but—"

"Katie," Gerry interrupted her. "D'you think we'll be tossing them out if the money doesn't arrive the moment you land in London?" His tone was gentle but teasing.

She knew he would not do that. She didn't want to be beholden to him for more than she could afford. It was not simply the money. That was not a thought that she could express. "As soon as we're paid," she vowed.

"I know, Katie. There's Peter, hurrying on his way. No one to see him off."

"I suppose there's too much to be doing at the bakery at this hour," Katherine guessed.

Peter was walking at a brisk pace, his shoulders straight and his head up. She wondered what he was thinking and whether he was counting every step forward as a punishment.

Gerry stayed at her side as the train pulled into the station, belching smoke and noise as it came to a halt. Katherine found trains loud and frightening. The sun was rising, replacing the darkness with a reluctant orb that appeared none too eager to rise.

"Likely going to rain," Gerry guessed, following her gaze and spotting the clouds already forming in opposition to the sunshine.

"Gerry, you must leave," Katherine urged. "You'll be late for work and your wages will be docked."

"I'll tell the foreman I had to see my girl off to London," Gerry said, daring now that her departure was almost near.

Katherine tried to smile.

"May I kiss you?" Gerry asked formally. "Then I'll go off to work."

Weakly, she nodded. She couldn't refuse him, not when he'd taken on the responsibility of her children.

His lips were soft against her cheek. He didn't presume to kiss her lips and she was grateful for that. Jimmy was gone now, but she still remembered the robust affection of his kisses and doubted that any man could match his big-hearted ardour.

"I'll write as soon as I can," she promised.

Gerry nodded as the throng of people waiting on the platform surged forward.

Katherine waved, then turned to the train. The secretary who had signed her up was standing on the platform, a book in his hands as he watched the passengers. He spotted her and nodded.

"Before five," he said approvingly. "Early. That's good." He pointed. "Third class accommodations, that way."

"On down," the secretary repeated. Behind her, the passengers who had tickets for the first class car were muttering impatiently.

Her face flaming, Katherine, carpetbag in hand, inched her way along the edge of the platform. Of course she ought to have realized that the Crystal Palace wouldn't be paying for first-class seats for its workers.

"I'll carry that for you."

Katherine, alarmed to feel her carpetbag being taken from her hand, whirled around.

Peter Edgewood stood beside her. She sighed with relief at seeing a familiar face in such unfamiliar surroundings.

Peter smiled back and glanced up at the sky. "I reckon we're in for rain," he remarked as he took her arm with his free hand. "They've roofs on the cars now. It used to be they didn't have to cover the cars for third-class but fortunately, Parliament did something right for a change. Open sided, though," he added ruefully. "I reckon Parliament decided that we're a hardy lot and we won't mind a bit of rain coming in."

He helped her into the car and followed her. The seats were wooden, not cushioned, but Katherine hadn't expected posh accommodations and sat down with a sigh of relief, even though her legs were cramped in the limited space between the seats.

"May I sit beside you?" Peter asked.

"Please do," she said, pulling in her skirt so that he could sit down.

His long legs were pressed against the back of the wooden seating in front of him.

Peter made a face. "I feel like a marionette," he said with a laugh, miming the movement of a puppet with his arms and legs.

"I suppose the railroad men didn't reckon on tall men having enough room to travel," she said.

"I don't suppose they care," he replied.

It was said with acceptance of the way things were and his words had none of the vehemence with which most of her Irish compatriots would have expressed the thought. She wondered what Peter's politics were. Half-Irish, half-English, he belonged to two very different worlds. Perhaps belonging to two worlds made him foreign to each.

He was an amiable traveling companion. When the train picked up speed, Katherine gripped the arms of her seat. A burst of air came through the open sides of the car, bringing with it not only rain, but a breeze that threatened to remove her hat from her head. She clamped her hand on her hat; it had belonged to Althne Murphy who no longer had need of it, but Katherine did not wish to lose it. It would not do to start her employment hatless.

As the train went along its way, swerving around the curves of the tracks, Katherine became aware of what sounded like a scuffle behind them. She turned her head to see a man who had risen from his seat and, from appearances, looked as if he intended to jump through the opening.

She gasped. Peter turned round to look. "A railway madman," he reported. "I've read of them in newspapers.

Sit tight," he said, standing. "We'll have to make sure that he stays in his seat or he's likely to get hurt."

Katherine watched in alarm as Peter, joined by several other men, moved to subdue the man who was standing on the edge of the car, his arms upraised, waiting for a convenient moment to hurl himself out of the mechanical contraption which was traveling at what even Katherine agreed was a frightening rate of speed.

She watched as Peter spoke to the man. She could hear the low, comforting sound of his voice as he reassured the frightened passenger that he needed to sit down and he would be all right. One of the other men who had gotten up to help, a burly fellow in working man's garb, took the seat beside him. "All right now, guv'nor," he said cheerily to the pale-faced man. "Sit down and if looking out makes you fear the worst, why, trust in God and all will be well."

Apparently Peter's reassurance and the other man's presence worked to alleviate the frightened man.

Peter returned to his seat.

"What happened there?" Katherine wanted to know.

Peter adjusted his trousers to accommodate the tight space between the seats. "It's quite common, I've read," he said with a smile. "Episodes of insanity on railroads when passengers are overcome by the speed and try to escape. It's all right," he assured her. "That fellow sitting next to him is watchful and he'll not let him bolt."

Katherine turned her attention to the rainy wind which was jeopardizing the stability of her hat as it dampened her dress. Peter insisted that they switch sides so that he, and not she, would bear the brunt of the weather's intrusion.

She protested, but Peter would not relent. "It's quite all right," he said as they changed positions. "You've had more than enough inconvenience so far and we're barely out of Birmingham."

Katherine smiled her thanks. God was already looking after her, by having Peter Edgewood as a fellow passenger. Barely out of Birmingham, traveling seventy-five miles an hour at speeds that the fastest horse could never have managed, on a vehicle which incited episodes of madness in passengers—what, she wondered, lay in store for her in London if getting there was so unpredictable?

ARRIVAL IN LONDON

To Katherine's relief, the rest of the journey passed without incident. By the time they arrived at the train platform in London, she had had enough of train travel. As they disembarked, Peter insisted on carrying his valise and her carpetbag. The secretary was waiting for the Crystal Palace employees on the platform. Katherine was relieved that they would now be traveling by a horse-drawn wagon at a more comfortable speed. The rain which had fallen as they left Birmingham had subsided to a gentle mist so that even though they all got wet in the open wagon, the rain was rather welcome in the hot August air.

The wagon drove them to a boarding house in what seemed to Katherine's awestruck eyes to be a very upscale neighbourhood.

"The Crystal Palace is being built in Hyde Park," Peter informed her. "It looks as though we'll be lodged not far from it. Close enough to walk."

He was correct. The secretary led the Crystal Palace employees to a boarding house. Here, the secretary explained, they would be lodged. The Crystal Palace funds, he went on, would cover the cost of their meals and their rooms. Katherine's spirits lifted at this news. If she didn't have to pay for a room and her food, she'd be able to send a greater amount of her wages home to cover Rose's care and pay the Murphys for taking care of Seamus.

The woman who managed the boarding house, Mrs Hufsnagle, was a sharp-eyed, spry elderly woman who appraised her new lodgers with a noticeable lack of warmth.

"Mr. Elliot," she called out to the secretary, "have you told your people what my rules are?"

The secretary gave a long-suffering sigh. "No, Mrs Hufsnagle," he said, "We have only just arrived and I have not yet had time to deliver the rules by which they are engaged as workers for the Crystal Palace. Perhaps you will be so good as to prepare luncheon for your boarders while I do so? May I use your parlour?"

The elderly woman glared at him. "That will be added to the account," she snapped.

"So I assumed," the secretary replied wearily. It was clear that he and the boarding house mistress had already exchanged words prior to the arrival of the workers.

There were eight workers who had travelled from Birmingham and would be lodged in the boarding house. None of them, except for Katherine and Peter, were from the Irish section of Birmingham and Katherine was once again relieved that Peter would be there with her. She knew that the Irish were held in low esteem by many English and did not look forward to having to defend herself against insults directed at her.

Although there were a sufficient number of chairs and a sofa in the parlour, the room itself was so crowded with portraits on the wall, bibelots, antimacassars, and assorted adornments that at first, Katherine could not see where they were expected to sit. Every available space on the mantel, the writing desk in the corner, the round wooden tables positioned between chairs and by the sofa, was occupied by porcelain shepherdesses, carved dogs or cats, photographs and painted portraits on the walls, creating the impression that the room was filled to overflowing almost before anyone had been seated.

Mrs Hufsnagle surveyed the new arrivals as they entered the room. When she spotted Peter moving to the chair next to Katherine, she charged, "Men over here," she pointed to one side of the room, "women over here. No mixing. I'll not have lascivious habits under my roof."

Peter's brows rose, but he promptly took his seat upon the chair directly across from Katherine. Katherine hid a smile and adopted a sober mien as she gave her full attention to Mrs Hufsnagle.

When everyone was seated, the boarding house mistress moved to a lectern at the front of the gathering from which point she could clearly see everyone. "I don't hold with this Crystal Palace business," she began. "It's nothing but a lot of foreign nonsense brought over from that German."

"Mrs Hufsnagle," the secretary interrupted, "we have already discussed your opposition to the Great Exhibition which Prince Albert is organizing. As we require lodgings for the workers, and we have contracted to pay your board which is entirely generous, I trust you will dispense with your personal views on the matter. Please proceed with the rules of the establishment so that I may proceed with the rules for employment."

Mrs Hufsnagle gave him a look as dark as the black bombazine mourning dress she wore.

"Or," the secretary went on shrewdly, "I can only assume that you no longer wish to avail yourself of this opportunity and would prefer that we lodge our workers elsewhere."

"You're all here now," the woman replied tartly. "I make it clear that while you're under my roof, you behave yourselves. I know that some of you come from those heathenish places where ungodly habits are acceptable. Not in my establishment! I'll have proper conduct here or you'll find yourselves out on the street."

"Mrs Hufsnagle, we really haven't time for this endless iteration," the secretary intoned. "The work is to begin immediately and the Crystal Palace must be ready by May. The industrialists and innovators of the world will come to see the marvellous accomplishments of the British Empire. This is a phenomenal event in the history of our nation."

"That's as may be, sir," Mrs Hufsnagle returned, looking, Katherine could not help but think, like a haughty black crow, "but I hope I am as proper a Christian woman as Her Majesty the Queen and I will not tolerate practices which might pass as civilized in other places but which are certainly not acceptable in this country."

The secretary made a gesture of impatience with the sheaf of papers in his hand.

"Shall I go first, then, Mrs Hufsnagle," he suggested with a glint in his eye that seemed to speak of recent battles, "so that you may instruct your boarders after I have done my part?"

"No," the boarding house mistress said in a rebuke as she circled the room with her gimlet gaze, affixing her eyes on each person seated in turn. "I shall go first."

For the ensuing forty-five minutes, while the secretary tapped his foot impatiently and heaved audible sighs of impatience, Mrs Hufsnagle delivered a moral itinerary of what guests where and were not allowed to do in their rooms, and what she proposed to do about any infractions.

Katherine managed to keep her expression suitably blank as she paid full attention to the lecture. Men were lodged on the first floor rooms, women on the second. There would be no traveling to floors or rooms not designated for the appropriate gender. Linens were washed once a week, at a charge already agreed upon with the secretary. Rents were due weekly, at an amount already agreed upon with the secretary. There would be no drinking of intemperate beverages in the rooms. There would be no smoking or cursing in the rooms, or in any place in the boarding house. Laundry would be washed at an amount already agreed upon with the secretary and paid by him. Soiled clothing was to be placed in front of the door overnight. Laundered garments would be returned to the front of the door within three days in summer, four days in autumn, and a week in winter. All guests were required to attend appropriate worship services on a weekly basis—

Katherine tilted her head slightly to see how Peter, a Roman Catholic like herself, was taking the news. But his face showed an impassive attention to the woman's instructions. Katherine wondered what he was thinking.

She was quite sure that Mrs Hufsnagle did not regard attendance at Sunday mass by followers of the Catholic faith as appropriate worship.

After the daunting train ride and the painful leave-taking from her children, Katherine was conscious of a weariness beyond anything she had expected. She longed for nothing so much as to be shown to her room so that she could be alone with her thoughts and the tears which waited only for privacy to be allowed to flow.

"Mrs Hufsnagle." Paxton's secretary interrupted with a stern tone which verified that he had reached the end of his tolerance. "These people will begin working today. There is no time for a diatribe on when and how they must attend to spiritual matters—"

Today! Katherine had not expected that the work would commence on the same day as their arrival.

"I won't house heathens," the older woman spat out. "I told you clear as a bell that I run a strict house."

"Perhaps," the secretary interposed, "the strictness of your house is the reason why you have sufficient vacancies in number to accommodate our workers."

He was impervious to the opaque glare that came his way. Paxton's long-suffering secretary walked to the front of the room with a purposeful air. Standing in front of the unlit fireplace, almost directly beneath a stuffed pheasant which seemed to occupy an honoured place upon the wall between a quartet of what were presumably family photographs, the secretary scanned the assembled workers.

"You are about to embark on one of the most ambitious projects ever undertaken by this nation," he intoned solemnly, fixing his gaze upon each of the workers in turn as if to emphasize his message. "Less than nine months from now, the Crystal Palace will open. The world will be able to see the vast array of technological innovations which bring us to a new frontier in science, industry, inventions—in short, ladies and gentlemen, you are part of the engine that will drive the Empire forward."

Katherine wondered if the secretary knew that among his employees were the Irish, who were not impressed with an Empire that retained its rule over a people who did not welcome the British on their home soil. Even the Birmingham natives who were not conflicted over their origins had a decidedly different view of their role in the Empire than what Paxton's secretary appeared to be promising.

She brought her attention back to the secretary. ". . . it will be a challenge to meet this schedule. That is why you will work six days a week, in daily shifts so that the work will not cease, even when night is upon us," he said, making sure that each person understood what this meant. "You will not be required to work on Sunday, so that you may attend worship services, see to your personal matters, and perhaps spend some time writing home to family members."

Katherine was aghast at this announcement. If the only day off from the work schedule was Sunday, there would not be enough time to travel back to Birmingham on a regular basis so that she could spend time with her children. What did he mean, they would be working day and night? Surely he did not expect the workers to go without nightly rest!

"Mrs Hufsnagle, will you be so good as to lead your boarders to the dining room so that they may have lunch before they begin their work. You may deliver any additional instructions while they eat," he said as the manager opened her mouth to resume her tirade. "There is no time to waste. They will go to work this afternoon and begin their labours."

"Come this way," Mrs Hufsnagle ordered, standing at the entrance to the room like a vigilant schoolmistress alert for transgressors.

Katherine gave Peter a distracted look as they followed the landlady down a carpeted corridor lined with more family photographs on the wall.

The dining area consisted of a long table with twelve chairs arrange around it. Katherine had a feeling that this was not the room where Mrs Hufsnagle took her own meals. It had a utilitarian look to it and except for a painting of Jesus driving the moneylenders out of the

Temple, there were none of the adornments she had noticed elsewhere in the house.

A maid with a starched apron and a ruffled cap on her head began to fill their bowls with soup. A platter of slices of bread was in the middle of the table, with crocks of butter on either side. Mr. Elliott surveyed the meal as it was being served.

"Bow your heads," Mrs Hufsnagle demanded. "Almighty God, protector of the Empire and ruler of the world," Mrs Hufsnagle said, invoking the Deity who, it seemed, had created the British Empire to assist Him in ruling the world she referenced, "fortify these workers with humble gratitude for being British. Bless this food to their bodies so that they may work tirelessly on behalf of the dear Queen. Keep them safe from heathenish practices so that they may worship Thee in Thy chosen faith."

Katherine bit her lip. It was not her prayer but this was not the time to voice her own religious beliefs. She had no doubt that Peter, equally silent with bowed head, was struggling with the same conflict. London in 1850 was no place for an Irish woman to declare her affection for her own country or faith. It was plain that while she lived in this boarding house, with her room and board paid by the Crystal Palace organizers, she was expected to give her allegiance to the country that had subjugated her own homeland.

Katherine had thought herself a foreigner when she left the familiarity of bucolic Ireland for the rough-and-tumble pace of industrial Birmingham. But at least, in Birmingham, she had quickly found the Irish neighbourhood of the city. Admittedly, it was the poor section, but the accents were the same as her own, the religion was shared and the nostalgic memories yearned for the same foods, songs, and heroes. Here in London, a city which teemed with people of all languages and religions and hues of skin, there was one class which dominated. It was not the aristocracy,

Katherine knew, although the earls and dukes of the realm were at the top of the ladder. No, it was the prosperous middle class, people like Mrs Hufsnagle, who dictated the standards—and the prejudices—of society. And to those people, the Irish were dirty rustics, who if they were not plotting anarchy, were sharing living quarters with their livestock.

Then Katherine was struck by an ironic thought. Prince Albert was royal and rich and the consort of the Queen. But to the minds of the average English person, he was a foreigner. Perhaps, Katherine thought, she and her fellow Irish had something in common with the Prince.

LETTERS HOME

Mrs Hufsnagle did not like the Irish. She did not like the Germans. She looked askance at the northern English with their accents and their rough ways, but at least they were English and they worshipped the God of the English. On Sunday mornings, when Katherine slipped out early to attend mass, she returned to the boarding house to a scanty breakfast. The others, Mrs Hufsnagle informed her with malicious glee, attended services at a reasonable hour and had eaten while she was out. Mrs Hufsnagle did not ask where she'd been, and did not make any reference to her choice of church, heeding Mr. Elliott's remonstrance that the worshiping preferences of her boarders were not for her to dictate. But she had her own way of retaliating, and a breakfast which consisted of the last piece of toast, by now hard, and perhaps a scoop of eggs or the leavings from the oatmeal, was her weekly vengeance.

Katherine accepted this. Lunch was better, in accordance with the standards demanded by Mr. Elliott. Katherine spent the afternoon washing her own soiled clothing rather than leaving it for Mrs Hufsnagle's critical eye and, while the garments were hung to dry on a line draped across her room, she crafted her letters.

Dearest Rosie,

I miss you. I am glad that you are in the sanitorium, where the doctor will make you well. Please take the medicine they give you so that my little lass will soon be strong and well.

I am working hard here in London so that I can send money to you for your care. When I come back to Birmingham, we will have a party to celebrate your homecoming.

Be a good girl and say your prayers.

My love to my little lass, from your loving

Mam

She could write at somewhat greater length to Seamus, who was older and could read on his own, unlike Rose, who would need one of the nurses to read her letters to her.

My dear boy,

Mrs Murphy writes that you are behaving like a proper little man and you are a great help to her, just as you have always been to me. Father Cleary says you are doing very well at your lessons, and you are learning your catechism. When I am at mass on Sunday mornings, I think of you in your good shirt and your best trousers and I am proud to think of what a fine little man you are. Your father, may God rest his soul, would be proud of you, going to mass and doing your lessons and obeying Mrs Murphy.

Mrs Murphy tells me that you have suggested going to work because some of the other lads in the neighbourhood are bringing in money to help their families. That is for their parents to decide. I am your mother and I do not permit you to earn wages at the textile mill. The money that I earn is going to provide for your keep and for our Rosie's care at the sanitorium. It is one thing for you to help old Mrs O'Donnell with her laundry basket, and if she insists on giving you a penny here and there, you have my permission to spend it on sweets, as long as you share. But going to work and giving up your lessons is not something that your father would have allowed, and since he is in heaven, he expects me to follow his wishes. Mrs Murphy does not want you to go to work at your age; she has told me that children are too often injured in the mills. I want my little man to grow up strong and healthy, so no more talk of earning wages.

Remember to write; the happiest of days is when there is a letter from you waiting for me when I come home from working.

Your devoted and loving

Mam

Her letters to Gerry were much more candid, in part because she was communicating with an adult and did not have to choose her words with the care that she employed in her letters to her children. Gerry knew the ways of the world and had no illusions that London would offer any charms which compensated for the separation from her children. He knew why she had gone to work with the Great Exhibition and he knew that she would be eager to return home when the project was finished.

Dear Gerry,

I hope that you are doing well. I thank you and your mother for the care you are giving to Seamus, and for taking the time to visit Rose as she mends at the sanitorium. I have sent my pay to Father Cleary by way of the priest whose church I attend here, and Father will be stopping by this week to give you money for the care of my children. He knows how grateful I am to the Murphys for giving Rose and Seamus a home while I am so far away.

I suppose London is not really as far away as it seems. But because we work six days a week, and long days they are, too, it's not possible for me to return home as frequently as I had hoped. I only hope my children will remember who I am!

I am grateful for the work and for being able to provide for the children even though I cannot be there with them. It pains me to be away so much; sometimes, and how you will laugh at this, I even miss the sounds of Clapper McDonough warbling through the streets on Saturday night on his way home from the pub, and the noise of Mary Maeve McDonough waking him in the morning with pots and pans clanging to punish him for missing mass again.

We live very proper lives here in the boarding house. I have told you about the boarding manager, Mrs Hufsnagle, and her rules. She does not like having us here, the boarders that she houses, but she covets the money that is paid for our board here, and so she glowers at us every morning. We are past caring about her silly ill temper, for we have very little time to bother with her. We are at the boarding house to eat breakfast and supper and to sleep.

There are many of us working at the Crystal Palace. Peter, the baker's son—but of course, you know who he is—is one of the men on the construction crew and they work very long hours in a great rush, for the Exhibition must open on time. They have a rather stern foreman, a Mr. Brown, who is not a very pleasant-tempered sort.

I am working in the greenhouse where the plants are growing that will be placed in the Crystal Palace to beautify the exhibitions. It is very hot inside the greenhouse, as you can imagine. It's like working inside a tea kettle! I fancy the explorers who travel the jungles and continents of the world must encounter such hot, humid conditions and perhaps they are used to it. We are not and I vow that the happiest part of my day is when I return—sometimes at night, we work for so long—to my room and fill the basin with water to wash in.

We have been told that it will be our task to see that the plants designated for placing in the Exhibition must be tended to as carefully as if they were precious jewels, for the appearance of the displays must be pleasing to the eye. I am told that one of the exhibits will be of a cotton mill. Imagine that, a cotton mill demonstration inside the Crystal Palace. I cannot think the addition of plants will contribute to a very authentic replica of a mill, but it will not be up to me to impart the truth of mill work to those who pay to see the exhibits.

The mention of the mill reminds me to thank you for discouraging Seamus from taking a job at the textile mill. I have explained to him that the reason I am here, and he is there with you, is so that I can pay for his keep and not need him to work. I am grateful to you and your mother for being firm on this point. I could not bear the thought of my little man suffering an injury and me so far that I could not be at his side. It is hard enough being apart from Rosie while she is getting treatment, but I am comforted to know that you and your mother are visiting her to cheer her up.

How is Finola? Are she and young James Ryan wed yet? I wish I could be there to celebrate with all of you. Sometimes, all that is familiar to me seems very far away and I am so sick for home that I very nearly wake up in the morning vowing that with my next week's wages, I shall buy a ticket back to Birmingham.

But of course I will not. I am only able to pay for Rose's treatment because of the work I have here, and I am so very grateful to you for letting me know about it. For all that I miss my dear little ones, and my friends, and all that is familiar to me of home, I can see that God has provided for me in this way.

Father Gallagher at St. Cecelia's Church here is very helpful. He sees to it that my wages are sent from me to Father Cleary. I would not know how to manage it otherwise. London makes me very aware that I am no more than an Irish country girl and I am in a foreign place.

Katherine was about to write that the only connection she had with home was Peter, but she paused with her pen above the paper. She decided not to write any more about Peter for fear that Gerry might take the wrong meaning from the mention.

It was true, though, that if not for Peter, she would have found herself feeling very isolated. The women who worked in the greenhouse had found their fellow Birminghamites and they shared a camaraderie based on the similarities in their backgrounds. Katherine knew of several other women from Ireland who laboured in the greenhouse, but they were from the Belfast area, not the Dublin region, and there was only suspicion and distrust between the two, so she kept to herself. If not for Peter, and the brief conversations they shared now and then, she would have felt very lonely indeed.

Instead, she wrote,

I shall close for now. I look forward to hearing from you with the news about my children. Please give my warmest greetings to your mother and your brother and sisters. I pray that the Blessed Virgin will keep each one safe and well.

Your friend,

Katherine

She suspected that Gerry would have preferred a more promising and intimate close to her letter. But grateful though she was to him and his mother for taking on the responsibility of looking after her children, Katherine did not want Gerry to assume that her feelings had changed. She remained Jimmy Foley's wife, regardless of her widowed state. Gerry Murphy was a friend and a good one, but no more. Her children were Jimmy Foley's offspring and as grateful as she was to the Murphys for looking after Seamus and Rosie, they would remain Foleys.

Her final letter was to Father Cleary, who had willingly taken on the role of intermediary for her while she was away.

Dear Father Cleary,

I have given my wages to Father Gallagher and he will be sending them to you this week. Please deliver the money that is owed to the sanitorium on my behalf; the Murphys tell me that Rosie is getting excellent care and is stronger, and coughing less from the treatment she is receiving.

Please, if you will, deliver payment to the Murphys, as you have been doing. They are providing for Seamus and visiting Rosie, and I am very fortunate to know that my children are safe in their hands.

Thank you for agreeing to put aside some of the pay to save for me. When I return to Birmingham from London, I hope to have enough saved up so that I may afford better lodgings. Our meals and board are provided for us here and not taken out of our pay, and so I am able to keep only a little with me for what I need.

We are not ill treated by our employer. It is only that the pace is very rushed. Peter Edgewood is working on building the Crystal Palace and those men work extremely hard, hurrying to get the Palace built by the spring, when it will open.

Thank you for continuing to provide me with the news about Seamus and his progress with his lessons and his catechism. He wanted to find work in the textile mill so that he could help with the expenses. The Murphys assured him that he doesn't need to work in the mill, it's so very hard on children. They alerted me to his desire and I have told him that he is not to do that. I hope that you will also encourage him to put his mind on his school work and his catechism. My Jimmy wanted his children to have the learning he was never able to receive and I intend to honour their father's hopes for them. When I am back in Birmingham, I shall begin to look for an apprenticeship for Seamus so that he may learn a worthwhile trade.

Thank you for all that you are doing while I am away from my children and my home.

Your obedient and faithful

Katharine Foley

LIFE IN THE BOARDING HOUSE

The vastness of the space that would eventually become the Crystal Palace was daunting. How on earth, Katherine wondered as she listened to the instructions given by the greenhouse manager who would be providing the plants for the structure, could they ever hope to fill such a space with the plants that would embellish the displays without getting in the way? But before then, how would she and the other women assigned to the gardening detail be able to tend the plants so that they were robust and in bloom through the winter, then ready for the spring opening of the Great Exhibition?

The numbers alone were more than she could absorb. Peter, who was working on the construction of the edifice, shared them with her one warm evening as they walked home together from their shift. It was a long walk, but after so long confined inside the steamy greenhouse, tending to the arrays of plants, Katherine welcomed the exercise. Even though London was in the midst of a hot late summer, there was a breeze to relieve the heat of the day. Peter, too, enjoyed the walk, and the pair of them welcomed the freedom of being in the company of another who thought fondly of lush green hills and thick green grass, and misty weather of what was, in Ireland, a "soft" day.

"Five thousand workers," Peter marvelled as they walked along the sidewalk, careful to stay far from the boundary of the street where the horses, not so well trained as the ones in Hyde Park, treated the crowded streets of the rough section of London with as much license as did the women emptying chamber pots or the drunks who, having overindulged, emptied their bellies with abandon. "We'll be installing eighteen thousand glass panels a week. Can you think of it?"

Katherine could not, and said as much. She longed to return to her room, to the pitcher of water she would pour into a basin for washing up, and then the blessed respite of her bed. She didn't even have much of an appetite after a day spent in the humid environment of the greenhouse.

"There's never been so large a building made entirely of glass in the entire world, or so Mr. Brown says," Peter went on. "I'm not sure if I believe him, but it's no good putting the question to him. He's not keen on what he calls insolence."

Peter left the topic of the difficult Mr. Brown and returned to that of the building. "It'll be on eighteen acres! I'm told there will eight miles of display tables on the ground floor and the galleries! When the plans were first proposed, the committee was vexed that three elm trees would need to be cut down. The design was altered so that the trees would be enclosed inside the palace. Can you conceive of it, Katherine: building a structure to include trees rather than chop them down? It's quite remarkable."

"You sound quite impressed," Katherine remarked. She wondered how he could maintain his enthusiasm after a day spent in demanding conditions. She had been told about the elm trees, and the need to save and tend to them inside the structure. A vaulted transept was added to the design so that the elms would be prominent in the final construction of the building. Katherine had no idea, and not any great deal of interest, in what a vaulted transept might be. It, like so much of her life these days, belonged to the enigma that was London, with its grandeur and its ambitious goals.

"Paxton is a genius," Peter said plainly. "Did you know that two hundred forty-five designs were rejected before his was accepted? And he finished his drawing in two weeks! Fancy that," Peter said in awe. "Two weeks to design a building where the nations of the world will come to show what they've achieved. 'The Great Exhibition of the Works of Industry of all Nations,'" he said, speaking the official name of the Crystal Palace. "It'll be a building, but with daylight inside. Can you conceive of such a thing?"

"When I think of our lodgings in Birmingham, where light is so hard to come by even with candles, I cannot," Katherine laughed. "But you'd best have a care if you're talking to any other Irish or they'll think you've gone over to the enemy."

"I suppose I do sound rather like I've turned my back on my own," Peter acknowledged ruefully, glancing at her sideways as if testing to see how she felt about his comments. "I don't work with an Irish crew, so I mostly keep my mouth shut."

Katherine nodded. She did the same and the sense of isolation that she felt as a result made her days feel rather lonely. It was only when she and Peter walked home like this that she could relax and be herself. "In Birmingham," she said, "we have our own folks around. And our own shops," she added. "And bakery. Have you heard from your family? How is the bakery faring with you here?"

"Well enough, with my wages," Peter answered. "It's helping with the rent. I don't mind," he said hastily, as if he feared he sounded like he was complaining. "Some of the lads back home talked of going to America," Peter recalled. "I can't fault them," he acknowledged hesitantly. "Only—for me, Ireland is home. Even if I'm not there, it's still home. I still remember it, though we've been in England for almost eight years."

Peter was her age, Katherine knew, and at twenty-four, he'd certainly be able to vividly recall the homeland he and his family had left when he was sixteen.

Katherine remembered the talk of emigrating going on in her village as well. But instead, most of them had gone to England. It was closer, even if it was English. She didn't think she could ever abandon her hopes of one day returning to Ireland, even if such a hope was forlorn. What was there in Ireland? Only the beauty of the land, and the beloved familiarity of the people, the food, the language itself. But with so many Irish losing their farms or being turned out onto the street as the famine raged, Ireland was not a place where she could provide for her children. But of all places on earth, it was where she wanted them to grow up. Somehow, that was an integral cog in the process that had brought her to London so that she could see that they were cared for in Birmingham.

A lazy breeze eddied down the street as they were walking, Strands of loose hair blew into Katherine's face. Her dress billowed slightly around her legs as the breeze grew stronger. Peter grabbed hold of his cap.

"I reckon it's going to rain," he said philosophically.

"We'd better hurry, then," Katherine suggested. "I shudder to think at what Mrs Hufsnagle will say if we both come in together, dripping wet."

"She'll likely make us stand outside lest we leave her carpets damp," Peter agreed.

"What a sour face she has. It's near as grim as that stuffed bird that's mounted over the mantel."

The pair laughed, sharing the reaction to the preserved pheasant which held such an honoured spot in their landlady's parlour.

They were nearing the boarding house now. By tacit agreement, the pair separated so that they would arrive at their destination by different routes and at different times. Neither wanted to exacerbate comment on their friendship, which could so easily be misconstrued given Mrs Hufsnagle's dire warnings about the separation of the genders in her establishment. Peter turned down a side street so that he could circle around the block and arrive a few minutes after Katherine, who would proceed directly to the front door.

Katherine smelled the odour of onions cooking as she opened the door into the entrance room where, in inclement weather, tenants were expected to divest themselves of sodden outerwear and shoes. The rain which threatened had not yet fallen and so Katherine was free to take off her hat and shawl and go to the dining room.

The other boarders were already seated and eating their meal. Mrs Hufsnagle, who presided over the table and read from the newspaper while the boarders ate, interrupted herself to greet Katherine with her usual message. "Those who come late get the leavings," she barked.

Katherine simply nodded. The reason that the other boarders were first at the dining table was because they shared the cost of a cab to bring them from Hyde Park to the boarding house. Katherine had not been invited to join them in this conveyance. As she preferred to save her money for her children, she found the walk the better choice. It offered the pleasure of exercise in the fresh air and the uncomplicated enjoyment of Peter's amiable company.

Mindful that the meal offerings of bread, baked onion and jellied eels needed to stretch to include Peter, who would be arriving soon, Katherine put moderate portions on her plate. She poured tea into her cup, bowed her head for a swift and silent prayer, conscious that the landlady was observing her for any signs of what she called Papistry, and picked up her fork just as the front door could be heard to open.

In a few moments, Peter appeared, nodded his greeting to the assembly, and went to the sideboard where the food awaited.

Mrs Hufsnagle, who had been reading an article about the Prime Minister, abruptly switched to a different story. "Trouble Brewing in Ireland" she recited, her dolorous voice now imbued with a spark of vigour. Articles condemning the Irish were a favourite topic for the landlady's meal time recitation although only two of her boarders were Irish and neither had any republican associations.

As she read, she looked up over the edge of the newspaper like a sentry alert for enemy combatants, watching as Peter sat down on the men's side of the table, his head bowed, avoiding eye contact.

"Trouble Brewing in Ireland," she repeated meaningfully, emphasizing the word Ireland as if by doing so, she could provide condemning evidence against her two Irish boarders.

Katherine forced herself to shut her ears to the woman's malice. There was more to being Irish than republican sentiment and a desire for independence, but she was not about to engage in any such conversation at this table and she knew that Peter, now methodically chewing his food, his gaze intent upon his plate, felt the same.

Failing to rouse a response from her Irish boarders, Mrs Hufsnagle finished the article with a lack of zest and then returned to reading about Parliament. Katherine wondered if any of the boarders, even the English ones, bothered to listen to her.

Did anyone in Parliament understand, Katherine wondered that night when she lay in her bed, so tired and stiff from the day's work that her body seemed to bar sleep from coming, how poor people lived? What did laws matter when a poor widow needed to earn enough to pay for her daughter to get proper care for a lung complaint? Or when an honest young man had to leave his family's business in order to earn enough for them to pay the rent in which the business was housed? Members of Parliament, with their laws and debates, what did they know?

And women like Mrs Hufsnagle, so rooted to her conviction that England and the English were the mirror of God Almighty and that the Irish were banished to the fires of hellfire for the sin of not being English and Protestant—did they ever listen to the scriptures read in their churches and heed the words of Jesus, who did not despise the poor?

Katherine felt her isolation keenly. At least in Birmingham, squalid, smoky, noisy Birmingham, she was with others who were poor. She had the consolation of living in a neighbourhood of Irish like herself, folks who knew, as she did, that no matter how long they were forced by circumstances to live and work in England, they would always be Irish.

Perhaps, Katherine thought as she turned on her side in her bed, there would be a letter from home tomorrow. A letter from home always lifted her spirits and reassured her that what felt like exile in London was for a purpose that would result in good things for her family: a cure for Rose's illness; money for lodgings that had real glass windows to keep out drafts; clothes for Seamus, who was growing faster than she could afford to outfit him in new trousers.

Tears formed in her eyes as she thought of her children, waking up in the morning without her. Seamus would rise to the sound of Mrs Murphy's waking and eat the breakfast she prepared. He would run errands for her, play with his friends, come home at mealtime to the call of Mrs Murphy's voice. On Sundays, they would go to the sanitorium to visit Rose. Did Rose understand why her mother was not coming to see her? Katherine had carefully explained the reason for going to London, but did Rose truly understand? Could a child ever understand why a mother would leave her children?

Father Cleary had understood Katherine's quandary. He had reassured her, in his calm voice with the accents of Dublin as musical as church bells, that she was providing well for her children. The Murphys, he reminded her, were good people, faithful members of the parish who were hard workers and devout. She had chosen well.

Yet even her good choice, as Father put it, led to another concern. Gerry Murphy had been the one to alert her to the opportunity in London. He had offered to let her children stay with him and his family so that she wouldn't fret over their wellbeing.

What did she owe Gerry in exchange for his help?

THE ACCIDENT

The passing of summer and its benign weather gave way to autumn, with cooler breezes that, not infrequently, evolved into winds. Katherine had no choice but to buy a warmer winter coat to prepare for the forthcoming winter. Even though the greenhouse stayed warm no matter the temperature outside, walking there and back required appropriate outerwear. Katherine loathed spending any money on herself, even for something as utilitarian as a coat. She'd managed to find a pushcart vendor selling used attire. The woollen coat was rather shabby, but it fit her and it was warm. Katherine noticed the derisive glances the other women working in the greenhouse gave her when they saw her putting it on after they were finished with their shift. She decided that she didn't care, but her cheeks burned with embarrassment at their disdain.

"Don't mind them," Peter advised her as they walked home, their heads bowed against the blustery wind that blew brightly coloured leaves off the trees. "They're foolish if they're spending their wages on trifles. When the Crystal Palace is built, London will have no further need of them or of us."

"Then we can go home," Katherine said. It had been too long since she'd seen her children. She'd missed Rose's fifth birthday, an omission which caused Katherine to feel such pain within her heart that she could barely force herself to rise from her bed to dress in the morning. Only the reminder that it was because of her work that she could afford the treatment that was restoring Rose to health was sufficient to stir her. That day, she worked with a heavy heart and was several times scolded by the shift mistress of her section of the greenhouse for not keeping her mind on her tasks.

She had walked home alone that day because Peter's shift was working longer to take advantage of pleasant weather earlier in the week. There was a boon in the rain which had begun to fall. Peter's work crew had not been required to labour outside for extended hours.

"Yes," Peter agreed. "For now, we must do as we're contracted. The Great Exhibition must open in May of next year. The displays and exhibits are scheduled to come then and the Crystal Palace must be ready to accommodate them. We're already at work to construct a working replica of the machinery that's used in a cotton mill."

"Sure, and a strange thing it will be to see a cotton mill at work for folks who know nothing of the tasks," Katherine exclaimed in disbelief. Gerry had worked in a textile mill before switching to a glassmaking factory and he had told her that the enormous looms took up considerable space. He'd also told her that the din was dreadful; in fact, he had left the textile mill because he was sure he'd end up deaf if he stayed. He'd also told her the work could be dangerous, particularly for the young children who were hired because they were little and could run quickly in amongst the working parts of the machinery. But their size and speed did not prevent horrible injuries if an arm was caught in the workings of the loom.

Bitterly, Katherine wondered if the glorious exhibition would include children in the demonstration. She didn't ask Peter, although she noticed that he no longer spoke with such awe of the Great Exhibition and its ambitious mission. Coming home too late to avail himself of the supper that Mrs Hufsnagle provided for those boarders who were prompt in coming to the table, and leaving so early in the morning that breakfast was not served, greatly diminished the amount of time that she spent in Peter's company, an absence that she sorely regretted. There was an ease to talking with Peter, who had no personal expectations of Katherine. He thought of himself as Irish even though he had an English father, and his fondest memories betokened his Irish heritage. He, like Katherine, keenly felt the isolation imposed upon the two of them by their connections to a downtrodden country despised for their faith and their heritage in this hostile city.

Peter, alone, understood the mixed feelings she had about being away from her children. Gerry's letters to her were always cheery and encouraging but sometimes, even as he assured her that the children were doing very well, his words made Katherine feel as if she were in danger of being forgotten by Rose and Seamus.

Rose, Gerry wrote, *was fair pleased when me and Ma brought her a wee cake for her birthday. She clapped her hands as if it were the best thing she could have gotten, for all that it only came from the Edgewood bakery. Still, the lass is doing well, there's even a bit of colour in her cheeks, and the doctor told us that she goes out every day now in the fair weather to get a bit of sun.*

Almost as an afterthought, Gerry had added, *We tell her that you're missing her sorely and counting the days until you can come home. She'll be home herself by then and me and Ma will be sure to look after her in the meantime.*

Seamus was also doing well, Gerry reported. "*Learning Latin like a scholar, he is now, and Father says he's the making of a priest. I wouldn't count on it, though I don't say so to Father. Seamus wants to be apprenticed and learn a trade and make money, he says, so that you don't need to go off to London to work and he can help take care of you.*"

The rooms she'd vacated upon leaving for London were now being rented by a family from Ulster, Gerry said. "Him a drinker, sad to say, and she not what she should be, with three little ones forever looking like they've missed a week of meals and a month of baths, too. I shouldn't wonder if they'll be booted out before you're back home and looking for lodgings again. They've the look of a pair who drink their rent money, if you fathom my meaning. Not to fret, Katie, for when it's time for you to return home, be sure I'll help you find a place. Be sure I'll find just the right place for you and the children, and not far from your old rooms either."

What did he mean, Katherine wondered as she folded the letter and put it with the others that she kept in her Bible. Was Gerry simply offering to help her find suitable lodgings when she was able to come home again, or was he hinting that he'd be making a formal offer for her hand in marriage when she was back in Birmingham?

Outside, the noises of a city which seemed incapable of silence continued into the night. Horse-drawn carriages and cabs were forever traveling past the boarding house. The sounds of people who took to the streets when the night threw up its dark shield over their behaviour filled the air like they'd been waiting for daylight to surrender. Even now, with cold weather coming on, there were so many who, inconceivable as it was to Katherine, preferred the raucous company of others like themselves to the privacy of their own lodgings.

Katherine's tears wet the pillow as she lay in bed. Birmingham's slum streets were noisy too, Katherine acknowledged. But she'd been safe in bed between her two children, comforted by the sounds of their breathing in the night and the sight of their small faces on the pillow. She had not slept alone since she was a young girl in her mother's household and now, with Jimmy Foley dead and gone and her children miles away, the solitude was unbearable. Without even the assurance of conversations with Peter to keep Katherine from feeling like an exile, she found the work days isolating and the nights bereft.

The days turned colder and Katherine was glad of her second-hand coat, however shabby it might be, as she walked to and from work, her head bent low to counter the piercing winds that howled, she thought, like the banshee of legend. She had no sooner entered the greenhouse and was taking off her coat when one of the Birmingham workers, Blanche Leston, a fellow boarder, came up to her. "Have you heard anything?" she asked, her pale, gooseberry eyes nearly popping with excitement.

"Heard anything?" Katherine repeated, "About what?"

Blanche had introduced the subject for the thrill of being the first to impart information. "There's been an accident," she said, lowering her voice as if she were imparting something too secretive to be shared aloud, "at the Crystal Palace."

Katherine's first thoughts rushed to wonder whether Peter had been injured and if that was the reason why Blanche was in such a rush to reveal what she knew. Despite the immediate worry for Peter's wellbeing if he was the injured party, Katherine kept her expression impassive.

"I've heard nothing," she answered noncommittally. "What happened?"

"You know they're building what's meant to be a working loom at that Crystal Palace," Blanche continued to speak in a low voice, but as she spoke, her eyes darted all around the greenhouse entrance, waiting for someone new to arrive so that she could impart her knowledge.

Katherine knew this. Peter had told her so. "Yes."

"Someone's been hurt," Blanche told her. "One of the workers. They've been working the men dreadful hard, I've been told," she said with a furtive glance around her. "I do hear that there's neglig—negli—something not done what ought to have been done, and now there's a fellow what's lost an arm and a leg, they do say."

Peter! Peter was on that crew. "Who was hurt?" she pressed Blanche.

"Dunno," Blanche answered. "I ain't heard, but turns out there was two accidents already from the men being worked too hard and the management in a hurry and not taking proper care for safety. Now there's a man dead, and likely a wife and children left without a husband and father to provide for them," she ended her tale on a note of dramatic, if unconvincing, sympathy.

Peter! If he'd been hurt, his parents would not only be deprived of their only son, but they'd also be bereft of the wages he sent home to help pay the rent for the bakery. "Is it one of the boarders?" Katherine asked, keeping the emotion from her voice.

"Said I didn't know, didn't I?" Blanche demanded sullenly, annoyed that instead of receiving proper regard for having the information in the first place, she was being prodded for details she had no way of acquiring. "I reckon we'll be told. I don't know if they've taken the body out yet," she added ghoulishly. "The accident was early this morning while 'twas still dark out, them working all through the night in shifts like they've been doing. You're friends with that Irisher," Blanche said, "why don't you ask him. If he ain't the one what's dead, I mean."

Blanche turned at the sound of someone else coming into the greenhouse. "What's going on over to the Crystal Palace?" Molly Latimer, another one of the boarders, entered in a burst of tousled hair, her scarf tangled around her from the wind. "There's a crowd gathering."

Glad of a fresh audience, Blanche said, "Someone's hurt. One of the workers. Might be dead."

Molly gave a disdainful twist of her lips. "Likely one of the Irish," she said with a speculative sideways glance at

Katherine to gauge her response. "A hammer in one hand, a flask in t'other, that's what they do say. Probably fell off his ladder and if he's

drunk enough, he'll not be dead. He'll fall light, he will."

Blanche began to laugh, then, eyeing Katherine, thought better of it and satisfied herself with a soundless smirk.

Katherine barely recognized the emotion that rose within her. She could feel it coming from the very soles of her feet, rising like the sail of a warship when the wind caught it, mounting up through her body. Whether it was anger or fear or the stunned disbelief that her people were so readily maligned, Katherine didn't know. She put on her coat and went to the outer entrance, ignoring Blanche's query, "Where you going?"

She was going to see if the injured worker was Peter. Peter was not a drunk. He was hardworking and honest and if anything at all had happened to him, Katherine would not stand by and allow him to be insulted by two blathering women with their heedless and hateful gossip.

She didn't even pause to button her coat although the wind had grown decidedly stronger since she'd last been outside. She ran across the street and down the block and crossed more streets to where the Crystal Palace was still in its early stage of construction, an enormous glass shell rising up with a majestic roof on top, while inside, the building remained mostly bare.

A crowd had formed outside the frame of the structure; onlookers and gawkers, Katherine deduced. Not workers. She pushed through the crowd with a determination that would have done credit to a street tough and went to the side door. She knew the man standing sentry and she gestured for him to let her in. She had to see if Peter was all right.

The man hesitated, but something in Katherine's face must have either convinced him or alarmed him, because he opened the door with a wary, sweeping glance at the crowd.

"What's happened?" she asked him.

"A chap got himself injured."

"Which chap? Where?"

"One of the men setting up the cotton mill loom," he answered.

Peter was working on that display. Katherine, still imbued with the formidable spirit that had driven her from the greenhouse to the Crystal Palace door, thrust herself away from the doorman and hurried through the area.

It was easy to spot the loom, giant and imposing as it dominated the corner of the floor plan. There was a cluster of men standing in a semicircle as if they had closed ranks against outsiders. But still, she could see the figure of a man laying on the floor, with another man kneeling beside him. She caught a glimpse of a blood-soaked shirt sleeve and her stomach heaved at the sight.

Then Katherine spotted Peter's familiar figure, his dark hair and straight shoulders giving him an intriguing elegance despite his workman's clothing and sturdy shoes.

"Peter!" she exclaimed in relief.

Peter turned. "Katherine? How did you get inside?" He stepped out of the semicircle and lowered his tone. "Management doesn't want anyone to know that someone is hurt." He glanced over his shoulder warily.

"I thought it might be you," Katherine admitted. "Is he—is the worker badly hurt?"

"He'll lose his arm," Peter said frankly. "They're waiting for the doctor now."

"They're waiting? Shouldn't they take him to hospital?"

Peter didn't answer. He didn't need to. A worker couldn't replace his arm, but management could replace a worker.

"You ought not to be here," Peter urged. "Get on back to the greenhouse. I'll know more later and I'll tell you."

"Not if they keep working you the hours they have been," she answered bitterly. It was hours like that, and conditions like the ones they were under, that had put this unknown man into peril. It had not been Peter who had been injured, but what about the next time there was an accident? It was not drinking that caused these injuries, it was a reckless disregard for safety. People would assume that if an injured worker was Irish, he was a drunkard. Would the company defend a man if he was unjustly accused?

But Peter was right. She had no business here. She turned to leave. Before management came and spotted her where she wasn't supposed to be.

"I'll try to find time so we can talk again," Peter promised.

She nodded mutely. Peter's time was not his own. It seemed that even a man's arm was not his own, but was the property of the Great Exhibition, to be disposed of as the company chose.

ANGRY WORDS OF TRUTH

The doorman glared at her when he saw her returning. "You weren't supposed to go in," he said with a baleful expression.

"I wanted to find out if the man who was hurt is someone I know."

"Was he?"

Katherine shook her head. She didn't know who the man was, only that he wasn't Peter, her only friend in this crowded, noisy, heartless city.

"Well, that's all right then," the doorman said.

Katherine stared at him. "It's not all right!" she flared. "He's hurt. He's going to lose his arm. How will he manage then?"

The doorman gaped. "If he's not one of yours," he said, "then let it be."

Katherine moved past him and strode out of the Crystal Palace, wishing as she did so that she could keep walking until she was back in Birmingham.

The crowd had grown from just the brief amount of time since she'd last seen them gathered outside the Crystal Palace and now they were no longer content to stand in hushed patience. They were restless, hungry for answers, for information.

"Ma'am?"

She turned to see a short, wiry man with a cigar in his mouth and a pencil and paper in his hand. "Ma'am," he repeated, "what can you tell me about what's going on in there? We're hearing that someone was killed."

"Why are you asking?"

"I'm with the *Workmen's Press*," he answered.

She recognized the name of the newspaper. It wasn't one of the sedate London publishers who printed the sort of news that Members of Parliament read. It was a gritty newspaper that focused upon the struggles of the working class. Just the sort of newspaper that might actually care about what happened to a man who was in danger of losing his arm.

"What do you want to know? That a man is in danger of losing his arm? Does anyone care? An Irishman who is hurt while working is accused of being a drunk. No one will stop to care whether the men might be so exhausted from working such long hours that they're risking life and limb whenever they so much as climb a ladder. They're building a working representation of a textile mill, right inside the Crystal Palace. Did you know that?"

The reporter opened his mouth to reply but Katherine went on talking, fuelled by the injustice that the worker, even though a stranger to her, would face. "Do you know how dangerous the mills are?" she demanded hotly. "Little children are hired because the factory owners can pay them less. Never mind if a wee boy or girl gets crushed in the machine. There are always more children, the children of the poor, with parents who struggle to make ends meet just to put food in their children's mouths and clothes on their back. Will the Great Exhibition dare to show that? No, because the truth of the Empire's prosperity is that British wealth and prestige are built on the scrawny backs of hungry children, or men who are desperate to make a living. Will people pay for a ticket to see that? They will not!" her voice rang out, the accent of her home country strong in her words as she fearlessly indicted the rich and the powerful.

The reporter was writing at a furious pace while Katherine spoke so swiftly that she was barely aware of him at all. Someone was finally listening.

"Your name, ma'am?" he asked.

"Katherine Foley."

"You're Irish," he said.

Katherine, her hands on her hips, strands of her auburn hair coming loose from the wind that had begun to blow even harder, glared at him. "What if I am?" she demanded.

The man chuckled and threw down the stub of his cigar. "Miss Foley," he said, with a look of admiration that turned Katherine's glare to a scowl, "if the Emerald Isle has any more lovely ladies like you, ladies whose hearts are as passionate as their voices, I don't see how the Irish can fail to win their independence." He gave her a bow, which, although mocking, seemed to display his own disdain for the British Empire that she had described.

"There's no sign of that," Katherine said, suddenly subdued. Irish independence, that was the rallying cry of Gerry Murphy's mother and how many more back home. But independence meant more than nationhood and separation from the English. It would mean nothing to Katherine if she could not afford to raise the children she'd borne to Jimmy Foley.

The man tipped his finger to his hat. "My paper supports independence," he said.

Perhaps that was just as well, Katherine thought as she watched him retreat from the throng of people outside the Crystal Palace. The only ones likely to read a paper that promoted the independence of Ireland were the Irish themselves.

∼

The episode at the Crystal Palace was the talk of the greenhouse and of the boarding house. The injured worker would survive, but he had lost his arm and would be going home to Birmingham. There would be no compensation for his injury.

The fuse of anger that had sparked Katherine's vehement response to the reporter had fizzled into a numbing resignation of her fate. Her worries about her children were of no significance in a city which had no shortage of workers. If she, or the other Irish, or any of the people from Birmingham, were injured in their labours or simply chose to go home and leave London, the city would easily replace them with others from Ireland, from Birmingham, from the slums which desperation and poverty had midwifed throughout the realm. She did not read the article and gave it no further thought.

Until, that is, she was met at the entrance to the greenhouse by a stern-looking man wearing a great coat and a hat who stood in front of the door, barring her way.

"Mrs Foley," he stated.

"Yes?"

"Management wants to speak to you. Follow me."

"Who are you?" she asked hesitantly.

"My name's Brown."

Brown. The foreman who worked the men so hard. The man's hawk-like eyes surveyed her from her head to her feet. There wasn't much he could see beneath the thick winter coat, but his gaze left the impression that he could peel off layers of clothing with a look.

Why had Mr. Brown been sent to fetch her? "Management—about what?" she inquired. She was doing her job and working her hours. The workers would soon be moving from the greenhouse to the Crystal Palace itself, where they would arrange the plants they had been tending and look after them so that the greenery would thrive in their new home. The glass panels of the Crystal Palace would provide the light that was vital for plants, but they would need careful attention so that they did not wilt, or fade, or die. Was her work thus far deficient?

Katherine struggled to keep up with the pace of the stern man, who said nothing as they walked several blocks until he stopped in front of a three-storey building on the corner of a respectable section of the neighbourhood.

"In there," he gestured toward the doors. "They're waiting for you."

"Waiting where?" she queried, flustered by his tone and by the lack of information.

"Just go inside. They're waiting." He delivered one more sweeping scrutiny of her body and then turned away.

If he intended for his words to sound ominous, he succeeded. Katherine walked alone up the broad stone steps. A brass sign at the side of the doors identified the building as the Great Exhibition Operations Office. Katherine had given no thought to how the business of the Crystal Palace was undertaken until now.

The door opened as she approached it. A small, stoop-shouldered man in shirtsleeves and garters stood there. "Dear me," he said when she entered. "Dear me."

His greeting did not sound promising. "I was told to come here," she said.

"Yes, yes, so I should think you were."

"Why am I here?"

"Dear me," he said, shaking his head, his forefinger pressing against his chin as he surveyed her. "I should think you must know."

"Well, I don't know," she replied with more bravado than she felt.

"It's to do with the Mick Kiernan business," he said.

"Who is Mick Kiernan?"

He gave her a dubious and disapproving look. "Don't act as if you don't know. Come with me."

There were a number of doors along the corridor, all of them closed. She couldn't hear any voices as she passed the offices, yet the signs on the doors indicated that weighty matters must be transpiring behind them.

"Office of Industry."

"Office of Design."

"Office of Engineering."

"Office of Botanical Displays." Was that the greenhouse, Katherine wondered. Was this where the decision had been made to select particular plants and place them in certain locations?

"Office of the Press."

The little man walked swiftly past this door as if he had no wish to dawdle in front of it. He began walking so quickly that Katherine could not take the time to notice the signs on the other doors.

Then he stopped.

"Office of Labour."

He gave her a schoolmaster's glance as if he were warning her to behave. Then he knocked on the door, a single rap with his knuckles.

"Come in," directed a stentorian voice.

The little man opened the door but did not enter, or even allow himself to be seen by the occupants on the other side of the door. He nodded at her to indicate she was to enter.

She heard the door close behind her.

In front of her was a table, a very handsome looking table, with intricately carved legs that matched the carvings on the seven chairs arranged around its length.

"Mrs Foley," said the man at the head of the table.

He seemed to be waiting for her to confirm her identify.

"I am Mrs Foley," she replied.

"I am Lord Ardmore," he returned as if he assumed she knew who he was.

Why would someone with a title want to speak to her, Katherine wondered with a sinking heart. It couldn't be for any good reason, and Rose wasn't finished with her treatment. Katherine couldn't lose her job, not now, not yet!

"We are not pleased with your recent conduct."

Recent conduct? What recent conduct? She had disobeyed no rules. She had not even engaged in the badinage with Peter as they discussed their landlady's grim-faced parlour portraits. Katherine was always on time for work and never left before her shift ended. She ate her lunch within the allotted time span and was, in fact, one of the first to return to her tasks. She had done nothing to invite condemnation. Nor had she ever heard of Mick Kiernan.

"What recent conduct?" she asked, keeping her voice calm although she felt anything but calm as she faced this tribunal of bearded men watching her with polite contempt on their faces.

"Come now, Mrs Foley," spoke one of the men around the table, a ginger-whiskered man who looked to be in his forties. "You know very well what you've done."

"I do not," she told him, determined to show neither fear nor defiance, although she felt both.

"You spoke to the press," he said, his lip curling on the last word. "We do not pay our workers to communicate with the press. We estimate that you must have spoken to him for an hour. Your wages for the day will be docked for that time, plus the time it would have taken you to walk to the Crystal Palace. You are paid to work, not to exchange information of a private matter with a member of the press. They are disreputable men and you ought to have known better."

"You spoke out of turn, Mrs Foley," another man, this one a rotund gentleman with a waistcoat that strained across the swell of his belly, took up the discussion.

Katherine noticed that he too, like the first man who had spoken to her, bore an expression that she recognized. It was the look she imagined she wore when she was trying to cross the streets of her Birmingham neighbourhood while essaying to avoid the piles of droppings, filth and offal that were as much a part of the cobblestones as the people and beasts that created those offensive heaps.

Katherine straightened her back. She wasn't the filth of the street. "I spoke what I felt, sir," she told him. "I was not told that I could not speak. I was not aware that I was speaking out of turn. We were given rules when we began working. I have not broken any of them."

"We will be conducting an investigation of your behaviour on that day," Lord Ardmore spoke again. "In the meantime, you are forbidden to work inside the greenhouse or the Crystal Palace. You are not to enter the grounds during the investigation. If it were within my power, I would also forbid you from boarding with the other workers. Unfortunately, I was not consulted on that arrangement. However, you are accountable for the days of lodging in the boarding house while the investigation is underway. You will pay on your own. That is all."

There was no farewell or even acknowledgment that she was to leave. The men turned away from her as if she were invisible.

Katherine, her face flaming, walking stiffly to the door, fumbling as she reached for the door knob. When she was outside the room, the door closed behind her, she leaned against the wall, struggling to draw her breath. She was going to lose her position and Rosie wasn't yet free of the lung complaint that set her to coughing! She'd failed her children because she couldn't keep her tongue still.

A single sob escape from her lungs. Then Katherine forced herself to be calm. It was bad enough that she had failed her daughter. She wasn't a Fenian, but she was as Irish as any of them. She would not embarrass herself or the name of Foley by showing weakness in front of the English.

THE INVESTIGATION

Katherine put her coins into Mrs Hufsnagle's greedy palm.

"And for meals," the landlady prodded her.

"I won't be taking meals here for the time being," Katherine answered. She would not sit through another humiliating evening meal while the landlady, fairly steaming like a tea kettle before the entire contents were boiling, targeted Katherine, without ever naming her, in a diatribe lambasting the ungrateful Papists who came to England for work and bit the hand that fed them. Word of Katherine's interview with the newspaper, and the subsequent investigation into her conduct, had been delivered to the boarding house before Katherine returned there following the unsettling interrogation with the Crystal Palace management.

The older lady's eyes seemed to snap when she blinked. "You won't find a better meal on the street," she warned.

They were alone in the parlour. The others had gone off to work following breakfast. Katherine, unable to face them, had gone up to her room until they were gone. Then she'd gone downstairs to pay her board.

"I do not expect to," Katherine responded. She would buy food for the day from the ever-present street vendors who could be counted on to have hot meat pies and hot tea for Katherine to eat and drink. She needed to be especially frugal now. She'd saved up most of her wages, but much of that had been sent home to Father Cleary for her family's care. Now, with her future undecided and her present not at all promising, Katherine intended to eat sparingly.

The stuffed pheasant above the mantel looked as haughty as ever, its glass eyes fixed upon her as she stood before Mrs Hufsnagle. Katherine had never noticed it before, but she suddenly realized that the bird and the boarding house manager shared a remarkably similar expression on their faces. She had to stifle an unexpected giggle at the thought of the bird occupying Mrs Hufsnagle's body. Peter would have appreciated the humour but, despite his promise, Katherine had not seen him since the day of the accident at the Crystal Palace.

Donning her coat and hat, Katherine went out into the street, already teeming with activity. Except for the brisk morning and evening walks to and from the greenhouse, Katherine spent very little time engaging with the people whose livelihood took place outside, selling their wares to the workers who rushed by. It had never occurred to her what it must be like to earn one's pay by working outside in all manner of weather. She had not thought of it before but at least when she worked in the greenhouse, she was sheltered from the winds that sliced through the streets like invisible scythes. The vendors were bundled up in an odd assortment of garb, all colours, all textures, as they exchanged crumpets, roasted nuts, and soup for the money offered by passers-by. The aromas of the food were tantalizing to Katherine.

She paused before the street cart where a plump woman wearing what appeared to be several layers of shawls, along with fingerless gloves, was scooping nuts into a paper bag.

"Yes, dearie?" the woman asked. "You look like you'd do well with some of what I'm selling."

"Yes," Katherine said. "I believe I would."

The woman gave a gap-toothed grin. "There you go," she said. "Keep you warm, too, on this nasty day."

The bag was indeed warm in her hands. Katherine handed over the amount she owed, and then, impulsively, added a bit more to the total as she saw the woman's fingertips, red from the cold.

"Bless you, dearie," the woman said wonderingly.

Katherine smiled and continued on her way. It was, she knew, a frivolous thing to do. But somehow, she felt it was right. It ought not to have taken her until she was at risk of losing her job to realize how much other people struggled as well, even Londoners. Even the English. The poor were the poor everywhere.

Her sanguine mood carried her on down the street, until she passed a newsstand. Her attention was captured by the headline on one of the smaller news sheets for sale.

Accident at Crystal Palace

Injured Man's Sweetheart Says Workers Risking Life and Limb

Sweetheart? Katherine stood stock still. The newsboy, perceiving her interest, positioned himself in front of her. "Buy a paper, miss?" he offered, holding it in front of her.

"I—who printed this?"

The boy, a freckled lad of nine or ten, looked up at her with uncomprehending eyes.

"The paper did, miss."

"It's not true!"

His young eyes were cynical. "Miss, it don't have to be true to sell. Don't you know that?"

Katherine handed him a penny and grabbed the newspaper from his hands, then stuffed the newspaper inside the front of her coat for fear that anyone should see her with it and associate her with the headline. She turned down the corner and walked five blocks until she came to the church. She went inside.

The church was empty, but to Katherine, even a church with no one within its walls evoked a presence. She never failed to enter a church, dip her fingers into the holy water, breathe in the incense, make the sign of the cross before the statue of the Blessed Virgin, and kneel before the altar without being powerfully and mysteriously aware that she was not alone.

In the dim light, as candles flickered, Katherine read the article, This was not the newspaper of the reporter she had spoken with on the day of the accident. This was a different one. The article provided some detail about the worker's plight and the loss of his arm. The writer alluded to the comments Katherine had made on that day, specifically her remarks about the lack of care from the Crystal Palace managers for the safety of the workers.

Katherine could not deny the comments. They had come from her and even now, knowing what she faced as a result of her candour, she would not have taken them back. But it was the next quote that made her gasp, her hand to her mouth as she read.

"Mrs Foley was distraught because she is Mick's fiancée," explained Peter Edgewood, a fellow labourer at the site where the incident took place. "Naturally, a woman would be upset at the thought of Mick losing an arm. Can anyone blame her for her response? Mrs Foley is an honest, hard-working woman who spoke up in defence of the man she loves—"

Katherine crumpled the page as if she could obliterate the words she read. What would have made Peter utter such a falsehood? She didn't even know the injured man personally, wouldn't have recognized him if she'd seen him. Nor did she have a fiancée.

How could he do this to her? As if she wasn't in enough trouble with the Crystal Palace establishment, her name was now linked to a man she didn't know. In print!

Katherine cringed at the thought of who might read the article. Her serene humour shattered, Katherine left the church almost at a run. If she had to wait until midnight, she vowed, she would confront Peter!

It wasn't midnight, but darkness had fallen by the time she saw him walking along the familiar route they had been accustomed to sharing before his hours became extended. She had stood in the shadows for over an hour and had twice been accosted by drunken louts thinking she was standing there for—for—

She'd responded in a manner which left no doubt regarding such a proposal, and then she'd stayed, waiting, armoured by her outrage.

When she saw Peter crossing the street, she stepped out so that he would see her. His tired face looked pleased at first.

"How could you say those dreadful lies about me?" she stormed, pulling the crumpled newspaper from inside her coat and brandishing it before him. "I'm not anyone's fiancée and you know it! How could you do this?"

"Katherine, please," he said, holding up his hand as if he were staving off a blow. "I heard about the investigation. I know why you said what you did and you were right to say it. Mick shouldn't have been harmed like he was and it's because of the push to get the Crystal Palace up and running by May that forces the pace. But I had to think fast to find a way to come to your defence and that was all I could think of."

The night was too dark for Katherine to see his features but his voice sounded penitent. Still, whatever his reasoning, he had spoken a lie and now she was tangled in it.

As if sensing her resentment, Peter went on. "You're here for your children. If the investigation goes against you and you have to leave, how will it serve Rose and Seamus? Rose wouldn't get the treatment she needs. You're sending money to support them so that Seamus doesn't end up working in one of the mills. I thought fast and hard and then I decided that I had to speak up. I—you must believe me, Katherine, I meant it for the best."

Katherine exhaled slowly, not realizing until the breath left her lungs that she had been holding the air inside. Her shoulders sagged. "I'm sure you did, Peter. But what happens when others read about it? What if it gets around?"

"You simply say that I was mistaken," he replied promptly. "You can say that I'm a lackwit who is forever getting things wrong."

"You're anything but a lackwit," Katherine said.

"Katherine—" Peter edged closer so that they were almost shielded by the corner of the building where they stood. "I know you send all your money home for your children. If you need help—paying for meals and board, I mean—I can spare some."

"Peter, you have obligations as well as I have," she said tiredly, touched by his kindness but of no mind to accept charity she could not repay. "I've saved a bit that I can give to Mrs Hufsnagle, and I can eat from what the vendors offer. I'll manage well enough. I just hope they don't sack me!"

"I mean what I say, Katherine," Peter told her earnestly. "I'll help any way I can."

"I realize that you mean well, Peter . . . it's just so very hard to know what to do. I ought to have kept my mouth shut, I should have. Anger took hold of me and had me in its clutches. I was in a fury over the way we're treated, and the way the English think of the Irish, like we're dirt."

"Do you forgive me?"

Despite herself, Katherine smiled. "I do. It's myself I don't forgive, for letting my tongue run wild like I did. I've never done something like that before. You're right. I don't know what I'll do if I can't afford Rosie's treatment. She's doing so well, too. If I have to go back home now and take her out of the sanitorium, it's the same as if I've sentenced her to death!"

Peter took her arm and gently steered her out of the street. "You've said what you felt you had to say. Now it's up to God."

They walked back to the boarding house in a thoughtful silence. It was good to have Peter at her side, Katherine thought. He had no ulterior motives and his hope was to alleviate a situation that still threatened. Whether he had done so or not, she couldn't say. But his effort reminded her that, as much as she felt isolated in London, she had a faithful friend who was looking out for her as best he could.

Mrs Hufsnagle was waiting in the entranceway and when Peter opened the door, she pounced.

"Out late tonight, the two of you!" she hissed.

"Out late, Mrs Hufsnagle, but not together," Peter said evenly, with only a heightened colour in his cheeks to reveal his temper. "I work late, as you know, and Mrs Foley ... should not be walking home alone. The streets of London are not safe for a woman alone."

It was as close as anyone would dare to an insult of Mrs Hufsnagle's London and she might have responded, but Peter did not wait for a reply. Instead, he crossed the room and went to his room without a backward glance. Katherine, just as eager to avoid any conversation with the indignant landlady, began walking in the direction of the staircase.

There was no pitcher of water waiting for her so that she could wash. Perhaps the water had to be paid for separately as well as the board, Katherine thought defeatedly. She undressed in the dark so that she would not waste candlelight and got into bed, pulling the bedcovers all the way up to her neck.

If she did have to return to Birmingham, Katherine thought, she might need to borrow money from Peter for the fare. Father Cleary had money saved for her. It would pay for lodging, but not forever. She might have no option but to accept the offer of marriage that Gerry had so frequently alluded to. They would have to live in the Murphy's rooms; the children were already there, and if married, she and Gerry would share a room—.

She could not marry Gerry! She could not marry any man! She only loved Jimmy Foley, no one else and she could not betray him with anyone else.

Katherine pressed her fist against her mouth to silence the sob that threatened to burst from her lips. *Dear God,* she prayed in silence, *come to my rescue. If I can but keep my position, I vow that I'll never speak out against the management again! I'll be silent no matter what should happen. Only let me keep working so that I can send money home for my Rosie's care, please God.*

Her thoughts travelled along the rough road that had brought her to this place in her life. She prayed for the poor everywhere, English as well as Irish, who were at the mercy of shrews like Mrs Hufsnagle and taskmasters like Mr. Brown. She gave thanks for the kindness of Father Cleary, and for the Murphys and for Peter—

"God," she prayed, *"do not take Peter's falsehood amiss. He meant well, though it would have been better all around if he had not broken the commandment with false witness. Still, Thou knowest his heart and it's a good one."*

Her heart was still heavy and her mind filled with worries when she finished her prayer. Then she remembered her mother's words. *'As long as you have God in your heart, child, you're never alone, no matter how sorely tried you are. Life brings us tribulations but the good Lord will not forget us, and the Blessed Virgin will hear your cries'.*

Her mother was right. God was with her and she was not alone. God would get her out of this dilemma and Mary, Mother of God would see to it that she could provide for her children. The New Year was coming and, please God, she would be working again.

AN UNWELCOME ADMIRER

The investigation had ended and the Crystal Palace management, perhaps influenced by the sympathy that the news about the injured man had stirred in the community, had reinstated her to her position. They had even, she learned through Peter, given the injured Mick Killian a small pension. It was not enough to compensate a labourer for the loss of his arm, but it was enough for him to be able to return to Ireland where a man could be poor without being denigrated for his poverty. The brief spurt of interest driven by the article claiming that Katherine Foley was Mick Killian's sweetheart had blown over when Katherine, at Peter's suggestion, declared that she had no idea where such an idea had come from.

Christmas had been bleak. She was more careful than ever with her spending, but she'd sent money home through Father Gallagher so that Rose and Seamus would each have money for warm coats. She sent money so that all the Murphy children could have a bag of sweets for Christmas as well. But for the workers of the Crystal Palace, Christmas was no holiday and they spent the day as if it were any other.

The New Year brought with it a cold winter. Katherine had spent some of her hoarded funds on yarn and had knitted a scarf and gloves for herself, and for Peter too. Sometimes, if their work shifts aligned, they walked to the Crystal Palace together. It was too cold for conversation on those early mornings before the sun was up, but nonetheless, Katherine appreciated his company. The dreadful feeling of isolation that had held her captive during the investigation made her especially appreciative of his kindness.

She also appreciated his presence, but for an entirely different reason.

"Good morning, Mrs Foley."

Katherine gave Mr. Brown a polite but brief nod of greeting. Now that she was working in the Crystal Palace itself, tending to the plants, she encountered the foreman more frequently than when she was in the greenhouse. On mornings when she and Peter entered together, he ignored her. But when she arrived alone . . .

"Let me help you off with your coat," he said.

Katherine backed away. "Thank you, I'll manage," she said.

He gave her a knowing smile, aware that she never removed her coat in the morning while she was in his presence. "As you wish, Irish," he said. He spoke mockingly, his eyes roaming over her as if he had the right to do so.

Katherine hurried off to the crowded coatroom where the workers left their outerwear. She never brought anything of value with her, wary that with so many people working here now, there was no way to be certain that no one was a thief. She hung up her coat, nodded to the others as she left the room, and went straight to the plants.

Katherine had kept the vow she had made to mind her tongue and say nothing that could cause controversy with the Crystal Palace management. She refused to rise to Mrs Hufsnagle's insults and was pleasant and noncommittal to Blanche and Molly and the others working with her. The isolation eased somewhat now that more of the Irish workers were in the same location. They didn't work together, but at lunchtime, they could share a table, sharing their accents and their memories and by doing so, building a shelter for themselves in the midst of this strangely foreign place. The women's schedules changed frequently these days, as they were sent where they might suddenly be needed to add a hand to whatever building project was unfolding. Katherine, however, found that she was always assigned to work with the plants. She welcomed the consistency of her assignment, but was uncomfortable when the other women chaffed her about being the favourite. It was meant well enough from fellow Irish, but less friendly when it came from the Birmingham lot.

When the respite of lunch was finished, Katherine hurried back to her work. All of the plants that had been placed throughout the Crystal Palace had to be watered. Their leaves had to be checked to see if they were getting too little sunlight, or, implausible in winter time, too much. New shoots needed examining and nurturing so that the plants would grow.

Where to rotate them, and when, so that once the Exhibition was open, they would have proven their stamina and would be able to thrive without constant attention. And of course, the cherished elm trees needed attention to, ensuring that their new environment was not doing them any harm.

Katherine, with watering can in hand, went diligently to every plant on the premises. She was particularly vigilant in her care of the plants which were placed in corners. She had been given particular instruction by no less than the august personage of Sir Joseph Paxton himself on what he described as "the aesthetics" of the botanical enhancements and because those plants in the corners received an imprecise amount of sunlight, she studied them with an eye that was especially clinical in its perusal.

"Stand closer to them, Mrs Foley," suggested a familiar

voice behind her, "and let them find warmth from the heat of your hair colour."

Katherine, startled, jumped and in doing so, spilled some of the water from the pitcher.

Mr. Brown surveyed her with a critical eye. "I suggest that you wipe that up," he said, "before someone falls. We don't need another accident at the Crystal Palace, now do we? The management board might not be so understanding next time."

Katherine, avoiding his gaze, took a cloth from her apron pocket and, kneeling on the floor, applied it to the spill. Mr. Brown moved so that he was immediately behind her, looking over her shoulder and, she suspected, stealing what sight he could from the neckline of her dress.

She hunched her shoulders forward and scrubbed harder to remove water that was no longer there.

She felt a hand on her shoulder. "That should do it, I think, Mrs Foley."

He didn't move away. She stood up, uncomfortably close to him, the edge of her apron brushing against his trouser leg.

He smiled as if he knew and welcomed her discomfort. "Well done, Mrs Foley. You've averted any mishaps. For the time being. You know that I can be very beneficial to you. Or otherwise. Well? Do you know that?"

"I know that you're the foreman overseeing the staff working here," she answered.

"Oh, I'm much more than that. I'm the foreman who reports on the staff to the management board. They make their decisions based upon what I tell them. For instance, if I tell them that you're working out well here and not causing any trouble, doing your job, they'll have no reason to sack you."

He stepped forward barely an inch, but it was enough that she felt crowded and vulnerable. She did not look up at him.

"But should I find reason to tell them that I have misgivings about your work . . . that I don't think you've learned your lesson. . . that I think it for the best if you're let go ..." his voice dropped to a whisper, "they would act upon my advice. You do know that, do you not, Mrs Foley? Compliance is a far better choice than resistance."

Her fear and her pride prevented her from replying. She stood before him, head downcast, the wet cloth clenched in her hand.

"We'll talk again," he assured her. Before he left, he placed his hand on her shoulder.

Katherine stiffened, raised her head in response, too startled to mask the expression of anger in her green eyes.

Mr. Brown laughed aloud and removed his hand. "That's better," he said as if she'd done something that pleased him. "Spirit is much more enticing than submission. Although," he added, "submission has its charms as well."

She said nothing, keeping her face expressionless and her body rigid. She listened as his footsteps retreated, and did not look up for a few more long, weighted moments until it seemed likely that he would be gone.

He was. Katherine leaned against one of the elm trees, weakened by the tension of the previous encounter with a man she feared and despised, but who had complete power over her continued employment at the Crystal Palace.

When she walked back to the boarding house that night, accompanied by several of the other Irish women who worked at the Crystal Palace but boarded elsewhere, she was subdued. The others were merry, tossing banter back and forth with cheerful, often bawdy insinuations. Although all of the women were of an age, Katherine felt as if she were vastly senior to the others. They were not widows with two children and for them, this stint in London was rather a lark. They relished the better pay and even if they didn't care for the long hours or even the separation from their homes, they seemed immune to the burdens.

"Hey, what's got you so silent?" queried Annie Riordan, one of the Irish set, as they were known, who sat with Katherine at lunch. "You ain't said a word since we walked out the door."

"Misses it, she does," declared Deirdre Houlihan, overhearing the exchange. "She's that fond of those fool trees that she frets over leaving them all by themselves at night."

"Maybe," Annie suggested with sly insinuation, "she's missing one of them lads working there, eh?"

The women took up this line of discussion with enthusiasm, naming first one, then another of the men who worked at the site. There were many men labouring at the Crystal Palace, but in truth, the sexes did not mingle much for their tasks were confined to different areas. Katherine recognized some of the men, but others were unknown to her. She ignored the badinage as long as she possibly could, until it—

"What about that handsome Edgewood chap, Peter?" one of the Irish women offered.

"He's a right handsome fellow now, isn't he, girls?"

Katherine raised her head. "Peter and I are both from the same neighbourhood, that's all!" she cried out hotly. "It's foul of anyone to make more of it than that!"

"Easy, lass," Annie said, perceiving that Katherine was genuinely upset. "We're only having you on a bit. No need to be so thin-skinned."

"I'm sorry," Katherine said. "I'm just---I'm missing my son and daughter, that's all. These days seem like they go on forever." It was true that she missed Seamus and Rose, not having seen them since August, but her emotions were entangled in the web of Mr. Brown's expectations and her need to keep working to earn the wages that would pay for Rose's treatment.

"You ought to come with us," Annie said. "There's a tavern where others of us go. We raise a bit of a ruckus, have a few pints, tell some stories . . . your trouble is that you do nothing but work."

"I dare not," Katherine responded quickly, glad for once that Mrs Hufsnagle had such exacting rules for her boarders. "I'd lose my room for sure." They had reached the boarding house where she lived; the other women would travel on down more streets and blocks to reach their lodgings.

"Ah, well, 'tis a shame," Annie said, now in a hurry to be off with the others. "Tomorrow, then, bright and early."

"Bright and early," Katherine echoed, mustering a smile. She walked slowly up the stairs and into the boarding house. The smell of tonight's supper, stew by the aromas, joined with the sounds of spoons clinking against the bowls, ought to have conjured an impression of coziness. But Katherine knew better. Home was a crowded, drafty hovel in a Birmingham slum, a line of laundry drying in the main room, her children sleeping beside her in the cramped little alcove where the mattress lay on the floor. It was not here, with Mrs Hufsnagle evoking the glories of the Empire while her captive tenants pretended to listen as they ate.

Katherine was not hungry. She went upstairs to her bedroom and sat on her bed. The room was cold; frost covered the glass in the window, obscuring the sights of the passers-by in the street below. She took out the letters that her children, and Gerry, and Father Cleary had mailed to her, and re-read them. It was a painful exercise, for reading the words they'd written only served to make her separation harder to bear. It also reminded her that she could not leave here until the work was done and she'd been able to pay for Rose's medical care.

There was no one to whom she could reveal her plight. The friends she'd made at the Crystal Palace where temporary; when her time in London was done, she would leave them without regret. They were Irish and there was comfort in that, but that was all. She was too ashamed to tell Peter about the pressure that Mr. Brown was putting on her to surrender her virtue. He was a friend, but he had no children and no dead spouse to honour in memory. He would surely think less of her if he knew that she was even considering the prospect of becoming the mistress of a man she loathed. Father Gallagher, Father Cleary, they were priests and unmarried. Fornication was a sin. How neatly stitched were the edges of virtue for those who had no responsibilities to unravel.

If Mr. Brown delivered an ultimatum, submit to his advances or be sacked by him, she had no choice but to give in. Her reputation would be forever tarnished and her sense of self-worth destroyed. In order to save Jimmy Foley's daughter from dying of the lung complaint that took so many, Jimmy Foley's widow would have to sacrifice her virtue.

She needed to decide. But before she became a fallen women, Katherine wanted to see her children again.

A VISIT TO BIRMINGHAM

Katherine stood before Mr. Brown, waiting as he studied her.

"Letting you go to Birmingham for Saturday and Sunday," he said speculatively, leaning back in his chair. "You'll be missing an entire work day. We're rushing to make the deadline as it is. You're asking for special favours."

Katherine held herself so tightly that she felt as if she were encased in stone and aching from the burden of the weight. "My daughter has just gone home from hospital," she said. "She's better. I haven't seen her since August."

"I am of course moved by a mother's tender heart," Mr. Brown answered, his dark and malevolent eyes moving over her body like a man reading a map of a continent he longed to explore. "But . . ." he lifted up his palms in a gesture of resignation. "I answer to the management board. They will not be sympathetic, I regret to tell you. If I am to risk their displeasure, I must have something in exchange. Something that will make the risk worth my while."

Katherine's throat felt so dry that it was difficult to form the words. "I will work harder when I return," she told him. "To make up for the lost time."

"What use is that to me?" he challenged her. "You ask me to take a chance. What if you do not return?"

"I must return!" she cried out. "I need the work. My family —" she lifted her eyes to meet his mocking gaze.

"Yes, of course, but when you return to the bosom of your family," he countered, his eyes boldly fixed upon the bodice of her dress, "who is to say that you will not decide to stay?"

"I will come back, I swear it, I swear by the—" she was about to swear by Jimmy's memory but stopped. "I have no choice but to return," she said dully. "My daughter is home, but she is still recovering. I must return to London so that I can afford the medicines she needs. Please, Mr. Brown, let me visit my family!"

Mr. Brown stood up. He rounded the edges of his desk with a swagger that seemed implausible given the small confines of his office. He stood before her, and although he was dressed in a black frock coat and black trousers, a white shirt that by its very colour made a mockery of the worn and shabby shirtsleeves of the labourers outside his office, and a formal cravat, he emanated a maleness that by his proximity was an affront.

"I will grant your request," he said. "But I will expect to be recompensed for your absence when you return."

He didn't touch her. Still, as his eyes roamed across the contours of her face, resting upon her lips with such familiarity that she almost felt the pressure of his mouth against hers, Katherine's skin felt the force of unwelcome caresses. She didn't dare reveal her disgust for fear that he would withdraw his permission and so she stood, powerless in surrender.

Seamus abandoned his posture as one of the lads when his mother got off the train. He left Gerry's side in swirling carousel of legs and arms, his head thrown back in his haste, his gaze fixed upon Katherine until he reached her and she held him close. He was wearing new shoes, and no skin showed beneath the hem of his trousers, and his coat was wool. The hours she worked, the long days, were proven worthy by the sight of her son, inches taller than when she'd seen him in August, with attire that suited his growth.

"Sure, it's too cold for wee Rosie to be out," Gerry explained Rose's absence as he walked alongside her from the train station. Seamus was on the other side, his hand tightly clasping hers. "But she's waiting for you, and Ma has a feast ready for eating. I thought to invite the whole street, but Ma said you'd not want to be spending time with other folks when you've only the two days to see the children."

"I'm so thankful to your mother for all she's done," Katherine said with heartfelt passion. And thankful, too, that Mrs Murphy, a mother herself, understood what Katherine wanted most from this visit. She would of course be staying in the Murphy lodgings, her former lodgings occupied by other tenants. But she'd sleep in the same room with Rose and Seamus and she'd be able to hear their voices, to hug and kiss them and hold them tight so that the memory of these moments would remain with her when she returned to London and the payment of the debt that she now owed to Mr. Brown.

Mrs Murphy had a fire in the fireplace, and a pot of Irish stew cooking over the flames. The Murphy family had a nicer flat than what Katherine had been able to afford, and Katherine was glad, knowing that her children were comfortable here. Her wages helped enhance that comfort and that too was money well spent and worth the labour that earned it.

When Gerry opened the door and Katherine entered, Rose was sitting on a chair in front of the fireplace. She saw her mother and, like Seamus, ran to her. Her gait was slower and not quite steady, but she didn't have far to go because Katherine ran toward her daughter before the child had taken many steps.

Rose would not let go of her mother's hand. The little girl was very thin, and pale, but she was not coughing and the absence of that remembered sound was proof enough that whatever sacrifice Katherine had made in going to London, the results were worth it.

They sat crowded around the table that was too small for so many and always had been. But the bowls were heaping with the stew, and there was hot tea for everyone to drink, driving out the cold of the winter with the food and beverage on the table.

Katherine listened to her children talk over one another as they filled her in on their lives. Seamus recited a prayer in confident Latin and earned the plaudits of his mother for his scholarly efforts. Rose assured Katherine that she was much better and stronger; Mrs Murphy affirmed that she hardly coughed at all, and when she did, an onion poultice took care of it. Rose wrinkled her nose at the cure and declared it smelled bad.

Gerry kept the laughter going throughout the meal, declaring that they'd soon start taking the onions right off Rose's chest and put them in the next stew. He said that there was no way to be sure that Seamus wasn't speaking naughty words in Latin, for who among them knew enough of the language to be sure?

In honour of Katherine's visit, Mrs Murphy had bought a ready-made cake from the Edgewood Bakery. She reported that they were doing well, but missing Peter something terrible.

"As we miss you," Gerry said meaningfully.

What would he think, Katherine wondered, if he knew that she was preparing to return to London to accede to Mr. Brown's lewd intentions so that she could keep her position at the Crystal Palace? Somehow, she knew she must summon the courage to tell him.

The children stayed up as late as they could, but eventually, they couldn't stay awake any longer. The other Murphy children were spending the night with neighbours so that Katherine and her two could share the bedroom together. After Seamus and Rose were in bed, Katherine returned to the kitchen. Mrs Murphy had gone to bed, more because she was allowing Gerry and Katherine time to be alone, Katherine guessed, than because she was tired.

Gerry smiled as she emerged. "Sit yourself down," he said amiably, pointing to the wooden bench in front of the fireplace. The flames kept up a pleasant crackle that added to the coziness of the room. He'd brewed a fresh pot of tea and handed her a cup after she sat.

"It's grand to have you home," he said.

"It's good to be here. It's been so hard, Gerry, being away. I miss Seamus and Rose so much." She sipped the tea to hide the tears that had begun to form in her eyes.

"Do you not miss anyone else?" he asked lightly, but Katherine sensed that the question was not without significance.

"Of course I do," she said. "I miss being here. Birmingham is my home now, with my children, with you, my good friends…sometimes I feel that I can't wait another day and I want to take the next train back to Birmingham. But I can't do it. Not yet, not until the work is done and I'm not needed anymore."

"I'm hoping that you think of us as more than just good friends. We think of you as family now that Seamus and Rose are with us. And I—you must know how I feel about you."

She had hoped to avoid this topic, understanding as Gerry did not that it could not have a happy conclusion. She leaned against the back of the bench and looked at the walls of the flat. There was a framed painting of the Irish countryside over the fireplace, next to a painting of the Blessed Virgin. The Murphy flat had hardly any drafts coming in through the window panes. The bright rag rug beneath their feet had come over with the Murphys when they left Ireland, as had the dishes set out on the table for the next meal. The dishes matched, and the table legs were all sturdy and stable.

The children were content here. It was up to Katherine to provide an equally comfortable and safe home for them when she left London after the Crystal Palace was built and ready to open.

"Katherine," Gerry pressed, reaching for her hand.

"You wouldn't feel the same," Katherine blurted out, "if you knew what I'm going to have to do when I return."

Gerry listened as she told him of Mr. Brown and his threat. At one point, Gerry was so angered that he got up from the bench and began to pace in front of the fireplace, his hands balled into fists at his side.

"I'd like to get my hands on that blackguard," he exclaimed, his voice rising.

"Please, don't—I don't want the others to hear. I haven't been able to tell anyone. I needed to see my children, you must understand, and Mr. Brown, he said that if he gave me the Saturday off, he'd expect something in return."

Gerry sat back down and turned to Katherine, clasping her hand in his. "Katie, I have cousins in America. In Boston. There's plenty of Irish in Boston, they tell me. Plenty of work, too. We can emigrate, you, me, Seamus, Rose. Father Cleary will marry us and we'll board a ship and cross the ocean. What do you say?"

"Gerry," Katherine answered, her voice gentle because she didn't want to hurt him. Gratitude was not a reason to wed, neither was desperation. "You can't leave. Your family depends on you, as my children depend on me. Rose is in no condition to take such a voyage across an ocean, and even if your cousins would be willing to help us—"

"They would be," he interjected, "I know they would."

"Even so, who knows how long it would take us to set up for ourselves?"

"What difference would it make if it frees you from having to make a whore of yourself to a man who's using his position to trap you?"

His words stung. She knew they came out of his anger at the circumstances she was in and his resentment that a man like Mr. Brown could manipulate his authority in such a vile way. Nonetheless, the epithet stung. *Make a whore of yourself.* It was the very accusation with which she had tormented herself, knowing that submitting to his advances would violate the rules by which she had been raised.

"I know that, Gerry," she said, her voice a low, urgent whisper. "Do you think I am glad to be in such a predicament? I can't lose my job, not with Rose still needing care and medicines that I can't afford without the wages I'm earning."

"Then come with me and we'll go to America together," he coaxed. "We'll manage it together, you and me."

"What of your family? Your mother, your sisters, your brother? They depend upon you."

"They can come to America, too," he declared, caught up in his dream. "It would be better there than here."

Katherine shook her head sadly. 'And would your mother be able to leave Althne and Finola, one in the convent and one married and getting ready to have a child of her own in a few months?"

Gerry bolted up from the bench, "If you really cared about your children, you'd see to it that they needn't have cause to be ashamed of their mother!"

"Gerry!" Now she, too, was standing, the two of them glaring at each other, their whispers at odds with the vicious words that were being uttered. "I do care about my children. If it were not for them, I'd tell Mr. Brown to go hang! But I have responsibilities that must be met. I'm all they have; their father gone and no family but me. I couldn't have managed this without the help of you and your mother, Gerry, and I mind what I owe you. But emigrating isn't the answer and when you're thinking clearly, you'll understand."

"Thinking clear is no use to a man when he's in love with a woman who rejects a decent proposal of marriage but will accept a sinful proposition!" Gerry took up his cap and his coat and flung himself from the kitchen and out the door.

COMPLICATIONS

Gerry was polite but mostly silent as he walked Katherine to the train station. Katherine didn't like leaving on such a sour note, but didn't know how to undo the damage.

"Gerry," she began, trying to catch his gaze. He seemed to be absorbed in the people waiting to board the train but Katherine knew that he was trying to avoid a conversation.

"Your train will be here soon."

"Yes, I know. Gerry, I'm very grateful to you for all that you and your family are doing for my children—"

"In the name of God, Katherine," Gerry said in a voice that, although low, was vehement in pitch. His words left his mouth in clouds of cold air as he spoke, and his eyes, usually so merry, were bitter with hurt. "Do you think I'm not fond of Rose and Seamus? You needn't fear. I'll not retaliate against them."

"I never thought you would! I know how kind you are," Katherine protested.

"I'd like to be more than kind," he said, his gaze a blazing sword as he spoke to her. "I'd like to be their dad. I'd like to be your husband. I'd like us to marry and get away from this blighted place. Do you know what it does to me, knowing that I can't protect you from the likes of that foreman at the Crystal Palace? You say you'd rather be an Englishman's whore—"

"I did not say that!" Katherine argued. "I'd never say that and you ought to know it. I said we can't emigrate to America because we'd be a burden on your family in Boston."

"It's not that and you know it. There's your train. Write when you can. Me and Ma, we'll make sure Rose and Seamus continue to do well while you're in London."

Katherine simply nodded, numb from his harsh words. She knew he was a good man. But she didn't love him. She didn't love Mr. Brown either, but she did love her children. What she had to do on their behalf, she would do.

Katherine was already awake when early morning came on Monday, having spent most of the nighttime hours fervently praying that God would save her from the twin fears of losing her job and sacrificing her virtue to Mr. Brown. She had slept poorly; being apart from her children after the short, glorious time with them, made the separation even more painful. Knowing what she had in store if she hoped to keep her job made the walk from the boarding house to the Crystal Palace even more difficult.

To her surprise and relief, Mr. Brown was not on the floor when she went, pitcher in hand, to water the plants and the elm trees. She didn't dare ask what had happened to him for fear that one of the other women might pay too much heed to her interest and mistake the reason for it. He might be ill, she reasoned, or he might have been sent to inspect another area. It was best not to assume that the problem of the amorous foreman was solved so readily.

But he wasn't at the site the following day either, and she learned over lunch that he'd been sent to work in another part of the Crystal Palace.

"Good riddance, too," said Annie. "Him with his eyes what were forever peering down me dress."

So Annie, too, had been the object of the foreman's lascivious attentions. The information relieved Katherine. He hadn't pursued her because he thought her willing; he was by nature a cad who sought to use his power for his own lewd gain.

It was with relief that Katherine wrote a letter that night to Gerry, telling him that the foreman of whom she had spoken had been reassigned to another part of the project.

"My prayers have been answered," she wrote, *"for now I can keep my job and continue to provide for Rose's medicine and Seamus' schooling. I am grateful to you and your mother for the care you are giving my children. I hope that we can remain friends despite our disagreement when I came home. The Murphys are the best friends a widowed mother could hope for."*

She wanted to thank Gerry and his mother for the way they were providing a comfortable home for her children, and to assure Gerry that she hoped the wages she sent to him by way of Father Cleary were helpful. However, she was reluctant to remind Gerry that it was her money that gave the Murphys extra funds for firewood and meat that benefitted all the occupants of the flat, not only her children. She refrained; Gerry had displayed a prickly pride in their acrimonious parting and Katherine feared that anything more she might write would only worsen the situation.

Despite the disagreement with Gerry, Katherine was relieved that she could resume her work at the Crystal Palace without the shadow of Mr. Brown's obscene expectations. She began to share the meals with the other tenants once again, and was successful in shutting out Mrs Hufsnagle's newspaper reading as she ate.

Occasionally, she would meet the gaze of one of the other tenants and they shared the same expression, covertly, as the older woman droned on. She was not nearly as comfortable with the English workers as with those who were Irish, but at least there was amiability among them.

It was near the end of the week after her brief visit to Birmingham when she received a letter from Father Cleary. Her happiness at a letter from home quickly turned to dismay.

Katherine sank onto her bed as she read the message.

Dear Katherine,

It is with a heavy heart that I write to tell you that Gerald Murphy has been caught poaching and was arrested. I have spoken with Mrs Murphy, who is beside herself at this dilemma. Although I do not hold with breaking the law and poaching, I think ill of the authorities who think a man may provide for a family on factory wages. I tell you this so that you will be aware of the circumstances. With Gerald in gaol and no wages forthcoming, Mrs Murphy will be hard put to put food on the table for her family. I know that you are generous in the money that you send home to provide for Rose and Seamus. However, I wish to alert you that the situation may prove to be beyond the means of the Murphys if the law deals harshly with Gerald, as I fear it will.

I shall continue to keep you apprised of the developments and in the meantime, I know that you will keep Gerald in your prayers. Poaching is a crime, but Gerald is a good man.

In faith,

Fr. T. Cleary

Katherine did not go downstairs to join the others for supper. She sat in front of the window, watching outside as the dark London night cast its oppressive shadows over the streets, stretching across the roof tops like a hellbound creature. If it were daylight, she'd have run to the church to speak with Father Gallagher. But it was late and she was tired and the darkness outside did not encourage a desperate quest to church.

Katherine felt that this was her fault. Had Gerry's pride sent him to the forest to poach for meat so that he and his family would not be dependent upon the wages that she sent home? She had never regarded the money she sent to the Murphys in that light, but Gerry had become a stranger to her. Had she insulted him?

She took her Bible from beneath her bed pillow. The Bible opened to the Book of Psalms, the scriptures where Katherine, like her mother before her, most often turned to find comfort. The well-worn pages opened on their own to Psalm 46 and as she read, Katherine willed the words to go to Gerry, for, in times like this, she lacked the words to pray and trusted to the ancient wise ones for their comfort.

God is our refuge and strength, a very present help in trouble. Therefore will not we fear, though the earth be removed, and though the mountains be carried into the midst of the sea;

Though the waters thereof roar and be troubled, though the mountains shake with the swelling thereof. There is a river, the streams whereof shall make glad the city of God, the holy place of the tabernacles of the most High. God is in the midst of her; she shall not be moved: God shall help her, and that right early. The heathen raged, the kingdoms were moved: he uttered his voice, the earth melted. The Lord of hosts is with us; the God of Jacob is our refuge. Come, behold the works of the Lord, what desolations he hath made in the earth. He maketh wars to cease unto the end of the earth; he breaketh the bow, and cutteth the spear in sunder; he burneth the chariot in the fire. Be still, and know that I am God: I will be exalted among the heathen, I will be exalted in the earth. The Lord of hosts is with us; the God of Jacob is our refuge.

Was Gerry even now in a jail cell, awaiting the diabolical justice of an English court which would sentence him with no allowance made for the plight of a man struggling to provide for his mother, his brother, and his younger sisters? Katherine thought of Gerry in better times, his merry smile and his eagerness to help. It would have been so much easier if she had been able to love him, she thought, watching as a sliver of a moon appeared above the chimneys and roofs of the city, its pale golden light a reminder that God had not forgotten them.

By the time she had dressed for bed, Katherine knew what she must do. She would leave for work earlier than usual so that she could turn in her notice. She had to return to

Birmingham and tend to her children. The Murphys had enough to deal with now that Gerry was in gaol; it was not fair to expect them to look after her children as well.

The morning was bleak and the skies were turning from ebony to pewter as she left the boarding house. She was not the only one abroad so early; London workers started as soon as daylight gave them leave. The grey sky spat out tiny flakes of snow that swirled in the cold dawn wind. Katherine bent her head to the cold; the wind demanded submission.

"Katherine!"

Not expecting to hear her name called, Katherine stopped where she stood and looked behind her. Peter was running in her direction, his thick brown hair already windblown beneath his cap, his cheeks red from the cold.

"Peter," she greeted him. "I haven't seen you in quite a while."

"Yes, but I wanted to hear about your visit. How are your children?"

"How did you know that I had gone to Birmingham?" she asked curiously.

Peter fell into step beside her. "Word got around," he said evasively. Katherine knew then that he must have heard of her trip from Mr. Brown and her cheeks flamed, wondering what Peter must think of her. "How are they?"

"Well. Better. Rose is still very thin but her coughing has eased and she's home. That is, she's no longer in hospital. Seamus is doing well in his studies."

"Why are you walking so fast?" Peter wondered, remarking upon her hurried pace.

"I have to—oh, Peter, I have to go home!"

"All ready? You've just returned."

"Yes, but I—I have to leave. I have to! Oh, Peter, Gerry Murphy has been caught poaching. My children are staying with the Murphys, but with Gerry in gaol, there's no money coming in. I can't presume upon the Murphys' hospitality now, not now!"

"Wait a moment," Peter said, ducking into the shelter offered by a shop front whose proprietor had not yet opened for business. "Here, the wind isn't so sharp within. Now," he went on as if there were no reason for her to hesitate, "tell me what's been happening. It's been too long since we've talked."

Suddenly, the weight of the recent weeks seemed crushing. The strain of trying to evade Mr. Brown's advances, her resigned acceptance of her fate, the return to Birmingham and Gerry's bitter recriminations, and now this brought Katherine to the breaking point and she unburdened her heavy heart. Peter listened quietly, and in the shelter of the dark storefront, her back to the street and the passers-by on their way to their jobs, she held nothing back, not even tears.

"I feel as if it's my fault," she wept. "Gerry has been nothing but kind and now he's awaiting sentencing."

"He's not sentenced yet," Peter reminded her in his resolute manner. "Don't hand in your notice. You need the work, and losing your wages will not help the Murphys. This is not your doing. Gerry knew the risk in poaching. Still, he's never been caught before and he's not known to be one who flouts the law. That will work in his favour. Do nothing now. Promise me?"

Tears were streaming down her cheeks. The salt made her chapped cheeks sting. Even though she knew there was nothing Peter could do to help, she felt relieved to assent to his request. Thoughts and fears that crowded into her mind were eased by his composed manner.

Peter smiled and took a handkerchief from inside his coat. "Here," he said. "It's too cold out to cry."

She began to laugh at the absurdity of his remark. "I had no idea that tears wait for warm weather," she joked.

His eyes were kind as he watched her wipe the tears from her cheeks. "Tell me about the children," he said as they renewed their interrupted route to the Crystal Palace.

Conversation with Peter was uncomplicated, without undercurrents, She did not have to speak with a sentry on her words, the way she did with Gerry, so that she would avoid giving false hope for an emotion she did not feel. When Peter asked about her children, she was not stricken with a sense of her obligation to him; he simply wanted to know how they fared.

As they approached the Crystal Palace, spotting familiar faces among the other workers who were converging upon the site, she responded to their greetings. Peter did likewise. Katherine realized with a sense of revelation that she and Peter were friends.

Why it had taken her so long to grasp that fact was a puzzle. Perhaps it was because men and women did not share friendships; every step in their progress was one destined to matrimony. Peter did not make her feel as if she needed to remind him that she had been married to Jimmy Foley. She did not have to redefine her past in order to make pleasant conversation. She was a widow with two young children. Peter understood this perfectly. Belatedly, Katherine understood that her time in London, difficult though it often was, would have been far worse had Peter not come to work at the Crystal Palace as well. She wondered whether he would return to Birmingham when his work here was done. Would his parents still need the wages he provided so that they could afford the rent on the bakery? She wondered whether he longed for a life apart from his obligations. He never spoke of it and gave no indication that he resented helping his parents.

She had been so absorbed in her own matters, Katherine realized as Peter held open the entrance door so that she could go inside before him that she had given no thought to what Peter sought in his life. He was such a good friend to her. As the pair separated to go to their separate work stations, Katherine resolved that she would be as good a friend to him.

A CHOICE MUST BE MADE

Two days later, the mail brought a letter from Father Cleary with the good news that Gerry had been let off with a warning and was no longer in gaol. He was back to work, earning wages, Father Cleary said, and, the priest trusted, wiser in the ways of the world now that he'd been alerted to the perils of breaking the rules.

Katherine smiled at Father Cleary's astute assessment of the situation. He was shrewd enough to know that people who struggled to make ends meet were tempted, and the priest, although he would certainly require penance from Gerry, had sympathy for the privations suffered by his flock.

That was certainly good news. Added to the confirmation that Mr. Brown was no longer among the supervisors managing the women workers at the Crystal Palace, these developments certainly proved that God had heard Katherine's prayers. She sent Gerry a heartfelt letter expressing her relief that he was not to be sentenced for poaching.

Father Cleary sent me the good news, and I wish I could be there with you to celebrate, she wrote.

Wrapping a blanket around her shoulders, the letter on the table in front of her and a single candle providing illumination, Katherine sat by the window. She looked out upon the city landscape, where flakes of snow were falling, obliterating the dirt that coated the streets and creating, at least temporarily, an impression of a white, pristine world. Even though it was drafty, sitting so close to the windows, Katherine found a strange peace in this position. The streets were not empty; there were stragglers and revellers and drunkards who were oblivious to the cold as they sought the camaraderie of the bottle in the taverns. There were the homeless who would wander through the night, searching for what shelter they could find. There were the women who plied their trade in all kinds of weather, knowing that they would always find clients whose lust overpowered any thought of weather.

It was no different from Birmingham. It was worlds different from Ireland. Katherine watched the snow fall soundlessly and wondered if it was snowing in Birmingham. Her children had warm coats now, and sturdy boots. She sent enough money that the Murphy lodgings were warmed by a generous fire. Gerry was at home and not a prisoner.

In such a short span of time, Katherine considered, her fears had dissolved. Mr. Brown was no longer a threat. Gerry, the breadwinner of the Murphy family, was out of gaol. Her prayers had been answered. Prayers were answered by God, but even God used people to make good things come to pass.

Katherine picked up the pen and dipped it into the bottle of ink.

Thanks be to God that these things have happened to us both, she wrote. *As I wrote earlier, I am no longer troubled by the unsought attentions of the foreman. You are not in gaol. I think we must both be blessed by an angel among us.*

She was unsure how Gerry would respond to her words. But perhaps Gerry would know more about his rescue than she knew about hers.

Gerry's letter came quickly in response before the week ended.

I'm glad that you were not obliged to squander your virtue, he wrote, his quick, rapid handwriting spilling across the page as if his thoughts had flown directly through the ink,

Katherine recoiled from the words which assailed as if they were striking her. The tone was brusque, quite unlike the Gerry Murphy who had been such a good friend. *Perhaps you have the baker's son to thank for interceding on your behalf with the foreman, although I cannot think that he would have much influence so far from home. However, his English father's word carries some weight here in Birmingham, I have discovered. It seems that Mr. Edgewood knows the constable, and for some reason, decided to intervene so that I was not punished to the full extent. I cannot think why the Edgewoods would get involved in my affairs, for to be sure I am of no significance.*

Katherine winced as she read his letter. She had been so delighted to receive it but now, reading it, she felt as if she were being chided by Gerry, who, it appeared, still harboured resentment from their last conversation. If it was Peter's father who had spoken up for him and prevented Gerry from suffering the full punishment to which poachers were subjected, why was Gerry angry?

Gerry's message implied that the absence of Mr. Brown was due not to happenstance, but to Peter Edgewood's intervention. Katherine had never spoken to Peter about Mr. Brown's machinations; how could he have known what was happening, and even if he had, how had he managed to have the foreman transferred to a different part of the worksite? Peter possessed no authority and no influence in London. It made no sense.

Gerry was simply in a foul mood, Katherine decided, and he would get over it.

She went back to the letter. The next sentence made her gasp.

I have made up my mind. I'm going to America. I'll work hard and pay for the passage for my mother, my sisters and my brother so that we can resettle. There's no future for us in Birmingham, where we cannot stand on our own but must depend on others, so that a man can have no pride in his own manhood.

Then she read the last line. *My offer of marriage still stands. We can all be a family in America where we can make our own way together. There is nothing for the Irish in England.*

He signed it simply,

Gerry

Katherine pushed the letter away from her and began to pace back and forth across the floor of the small room. The dimensions of the room, which had never affected her before, suddenly seemed as confining as prison walls. Gerry, with his bold plans to change his life, left her stranded between the loss of what was comforting and familiar, although not passion, and the possibility of a new beginning in a new place. She did not love Gerry. Did that matter?

She had not known anything of love when she married Jimmy Foley, but she had fallen in love with him the longer she knew him, as affection had ripened into a deep and abiding emotion which had sustained her through the birth of their children, the death of her mother, and ultimately through the death of Jimmy himself.

Katherine faced a hard choice. Should she cling to the past that she knew, in which Gerry was a reliable mainstay? He was good to her two children and they were fond of him. There would be no adjustment to make if he became a father to them. If he became her husband—

Katherine came to an abrupt halt in the middle of her pacing. The window was in front of her, the door behind her. Gerry and the past, or what? Who was Peter Edgewood, the man she thought she knew who had suddenly taken on an unexpected, almost mysterious role in her life. Without drawing attention to himself or expecting gratitude, he had come to her aid when she was in jeopardy of losing her position after she'd given that candid interview to the reporter following the accident at the Crystal Palace. She'd feared that the injured man was Peter, but at the time, she had not imputed any motive for her reaction other than concern. She had not told Peter about Mr. Brown's unwanted advances, but Gerry suspected that it was Peter who had solved that dilemma. Without accusing her of acting the whore. She had told Peter about Gerry's arrest and Peter's father, somehow apprised of the matter, had used his influence as a businessman to bring about Gerry's release.

What did it all mean?

For the short term, of course, it meant that she had to leave London and return to Birmingham and her children. She could not ask Mrs Murphy to continue to look after them in Gerry's absence, for every shilling the family could put together would be needed for their own needs while they waited for Gerry to establish himself in America so that he could send for them. If she was not going to be Gerry's wife, then she could not presume upon the Murphys.

For the long term? To return to Birmingham, admittedly with her savings, but with no flat to live in, no job, no means of support, and the Murphys gone, and with the knowledge that she was closing a door upon a friendship which had brought her great comfort since her arrival from Ireland.

The Murphys were like family to her. How many evenings in the warm summer had they spent together, while the children played and the adults talked, reminisced, and laughed? The best days of her life in Birmingham had been shared with the Murphys.

Gerry was known to her, but America was a new beginning. Her children would not grow up despised for their Irish heritage, for she knew well that America had become home to many Irish.

Her children. She had come to London for their sake. She would marry Gerry Murphy for their sake as well. The decision was made for her. She would put in her notice tomorrow and return to Birmingham. She would use her savings to pay for passage for herself and her children. They would settle in Boston and work hard so that one day, they would have a better life than Birmingham could offer. Of what importance was love when her children's happiness was at stake?

The next morning opened the skies to falling snow but Katherine had no time to bother with the weather. There was much to do. She needed to pack her few belongings, then go to Father Gallagher and explain why she would not be sending her wages home. She would go to the train station and purchase her ticket to Birmingham.

First, however, she must hand in her notice at the office where, weeks ago, she had been reprimanded and threatened with an investigation because she had spoken to a reporter after the accident at the Crystal Palace. How long ago that seemed now.

She could not do that, though, until she said goodbye to Peter.

She cringed at the idea of asking one of his fellow workers where he might be; gossip moved as fast as a train and even though she was leaving, she did not want speculation to follow her.

But she was in luck, for she spotted Peter outside, standing beneath scaffolding, a shovel in his hand to remove the snow from the walkways.

"Peter!"

He looked up and smiled at the sight of her. "Katherine," he answered. "You'll catch cold, you haven't buttoned your coat." He reached for her as if he intended to do the task but then held back and gripped the shovel tightly.

"I was in a hurry," she replied. "I—I'm leaving London. I'm going home. I—I have to. Gerry Murphy is emigrating and there's no one to watch my children." She shrank from the notion of telling Peter that she had decided to marry Gerry and emigrate with him so that her children would have a better life. She didn't want Peter to believe that she had feelings for Gerry that were not there. Katherine did not ask herself why she felt this way. The realization itself was too unfathomable. Why should she not want Peter to know that she didn't love the man she intended to marry?

But she did have something to ask him. "Peter, is it because of you that Mr. Brown was removed from his assignment supervising us?" The query came out boldly, animated by her curiosity.

"I can't take full credit for it," Peter replied, leaning on the shovel. Snowflakes, delicate and pure, fell upon his brown cap, disguising its colour. "I followed your example."

"My example?" she repeated, mystified.

He smiled. "I went to that reporter you talked to after the accident of Mick," he said. "He was quite eager to hear what I had to say. When I told him that the foreman of the Crystal Palace was known for making unwanted and improper advances to female employees who were at risk of being sacked if they didn't comply, he knew he had a story that would strike at the very heart of the Crystal Palace. Prince Albert is not one to tolerate such dissolute conduct, and the management would not want to have such a scandal erupting just a few months before the Great Exhibition is to open."

"But there has been no story," Katherine pointed out. "We would have heard."

"After speaking to the reporter, I went to the management," he said simply. "They understood immediately that Brown had to be removed from his position."

"But how did you prevent the reporter from writing the story?"

"With Mr. Brown removed, there was no story," Peter replied.

Katherine's green eyes were bright with gratitude. "Peter, you've come to my aid more than once. I'm in your debt and there is no way I can repay you."

"There's no debt, Katherine. Your bravery was my inspiration. You were fearless when you defended Mick, and all of us who are Irish, and you didn't fear to tell the truth."

For a moment, Peter looked away, gazing over her head to the rooftops of Hyde Park where snow was falling. Then he met her eyes, his brown gaze so open and honest that Katherine felt as if she were glimpsing a private side of Peter, one which he had never revealed before.

"I have always been inspired by you, Katherine," he said, his voice very low, his eyes steadfast upon her face. "You never lose sight of what matters. You came here to work so that you could help your children. You didn't want to come, but you did. I—" he looked away again, then his gaze returned to her, hiding nothing. "I—I admire that. I would want to marry such a woman. Your strength comes out of your love. Any man would count himself blessed to have such a wife. I—I would be blessed if you were my wife."

She stared, not knowing what to say. Peter had never hinted in any way that he had any feelings for her. Katherine had only just recently come to understand what a good friend he was. But Gerry was a good friend too. How did a woman know how to choose a husband when friendship was the tie that connected them?

Katherine did not know. "Peter, I don't know that I could ever feel that way."

He smiled bravely. "I couldn't let you leave without telling you how I feel. Even if the feelings that I have cannot be returned by you, I value them. You must do what your heart tells you to do, and go where it leads you. I am always here if your heart brings you back here."

THE HEART UNVEILED

Katherine doubted that she'd ever enjoy traveling by train. Her train trips had always been prodded by difficult choices that had to be made. Nonetheless, she bought her ticket for Birmingham and boarded.

But with each mile of track that the train travelled, devouring the distance like a ravenous beast, Katherine felt as if she were being hurried into a decision she did not know how to make. Did she want to marry Gerry, a good friend, a good man, someone known to her children? Could she be a good wife to him when she did not love him?

Did she dare to marry Peter, a quiet, considerate man who had revealed his love for her today for the first time, hiding his regard as if it might burden her?

As the train hurtled across the terrain as if its speed was the only consideration of merit, Katherine recalled the first train trip that brought her to London. She remembered the man who had suddenly risen from his seat with the intention of flinging himself off. What was the term Peter had used to explain the man's behaviour? A madman of some sort . . . a railway madman, that was it. Something Peter had read about, he'd said. Passengers who were overwhelmed by the speed of the trains.

Perhaps that man, like Katharine, did not want to be forced by the speed of the train into coming to a decision which, too soon made, would prove to be wrong. Everyone seemed so delighted by the vehicles which travelled so fast and doubtless the Crystal Palace would have an exhibition of some kind which would display the wonders of modern travel. Katherine thought longingly of the slow, ambling donkey cart that she and her family had used when she was a child to get from their farm to the village. There was plenty of time to notice the beauty of the scenery and savour the fragrant smells of the land, and ample time, too, to ponder a decision.

Katherine was weary of watching from the train as snowy slopes and tree branches flaked in white vanished from view almost as soon as she spotted them. She was tired of haste and worry, of mornings when she hastened from the boarding house to the Crystal Palace to spend her hours watering plants that were captive indoors. So much hurrying had robbed her of the time she needed to notice the world around her: the gorgeous trees in autumn with branches arrayed like bouquets of gold and red and; the hushed solemnity of a street swathed in the darkness of a winter morning when the bustle of the day had not yet commenced... the quiet devotion of a good man who had been her stalwart defender without her knowing it.

She didn't know what she ought to do. Until, that is, the train pulled into the station at its next stop. Suddenly, Katherine stood up and picked up her shabby carpetbag. She knew what she was going to do.

Katherine disembarked from the train with her head high and her posture as resolute as that of a soldier. It was surprisingly easy to exchange her ticket to Birmingham for a return ticket to London, and if the railroad clerk thought her daft, he gave no sign of it.

When she stepped onto the platform of the London train station that she had left not so long ago, Katherine did so with a smile. This destination did not stem from desperation or need or fear. She was where she wanted to be.

She walked briskly to the Crystal Palace, her carpetbag secure in her hand. She was no longer employed by the Crystal Palace and she no longer lodged at Mrs Hufsnagle's boarding house. She would need to find a place to stay until—until—

Until she and Peter were decided on their future.

The doorman scanned her dubiously, noting her carpetbag. "What you 'ere for?" he asked. "You ain't working no more."

Katherine smiled. "Please tell Peter Edgewood that Katherine Foley is here to see him on a matter of great importance."

"'Oo am I to be takin' messages to 'im?" the doorman asked.

"It's very important," Katherine assured him, her smile widening as she allowed herself the liberty of being amused by this entirely unexpected turn of events.

The doorman harumphed and then he scowled, then peered at her from beneath enormous eyebrows which could have done justice to caterpillars. "I suppose," he said at last, "that I might do that for you. 'e's only just over the way there, you might as well go fetch him yourself."

Katherine darted into the door opening before he could change his mind. "You're very kind," she told him with another smile. The smile almost felt like it belonged to another person. How long had it been, she wondered as she followed the direction of the doorman's finger, since she'd smiled so widely that she'd felt the movement of her cheekbones as her lips opened? She'd been so fraught with apprehension over the worries of each day that she'd allowed even her smiles to be rationed by her reduced circumstances.

She saw him, taller than the other men around him, his head tilted back as he surveyed the framework of the doorway that was being installed. He was pointing at one of the corners, and the man at his side was nodding. They conferred with another worker, who then went off in another direction.

They seemed to be waiting for the man to return. Katherine decided this was a good time to interrupt, but she had barely taken a step forward when Peter suddenly turned as if she had called his name. He looked at her from across a sprawl of tools, cloths, and stools and then, seeing her smile, his eyes lit up and he walked toward her.

"Katherine," he greeted her warmly when he reached her. "You've come back."

"I only made it as far as the next stop," she confessed. "I realized that what I feel for you isn't appreciation for your kindness, or even gratitude for your help. When I got on the train, I just wanted to get off it. To come to you."

Peter's arms reached forward as if he wanted to embrace her, but then he paused. "To come to me," he repeated.

"Yes. I'll still have to go to Birmingham, of course, to fetch Rose and Seamus. They don't know you, at least, not really."

"They've seen me in the bakery," he reminded her. "I'm sure they have a favourable opinion of a man who sells biscuits and tarts." He was smiling; she noticed that he, too, now smiled with all of his face, allowing every feature to join in with the happiness he showed.

"I'm sure they do, but I want them to get to know you as—"

"As the man who will be their mother's husband, and who will stand in for the father who is no longer with them," he finished.

It was perfectly put. Peter had no desire to replace Jimmy as their father. He wanted to do for them the things that Jimmy would have done, had he lived.

"We've got rather a lot of talking to do," he observed,

"And you have to go back to work, I know."

"Yes. . . where will you stay?"

"I'll find a room," she said confidently.

"If you travel just a block up from here, you'll find a boarding house on the corner of the street. It's run by a very nice woman, a war widow. She has a room."

"How do you know that?" Katherine asked.

"When you were worried that you were going to be sacked, I did a bit of checking around. I found her boarding house and we got to talking. She's very kind and she doesn't have a great stuffed pheasant mounted on her parlour wall."

Katherine laughed along with Peter.

"And her rates are very reasonable," Peter added. "Let her know that your children will be joining you."

Uncertainty suddenly assailed Katherine. "Peter, what if I'm being hasty? I don't want to take the children away from what they know. They're comfortable in Birmingham."

"With circumstances as they are now, yes. But if Gerry is leaving for America, their lives will be changing as well. They'd rather be with you."

"I'll need to find work," she said, thinking aloud. "I've saved up money but it won't last long. I'll need—"

"What would you say," Peter proposed, his head tilted to one side as he framed his query, "to being a baker's wife?"

"A baker's wife?" she repeated.

He was grinning. "My parents want me to come back and take over the bakery. The bakery is doing so well that they've been able to put aside the wages I've been sending them. They wrote me a couple of weeks ago to ask. They'll be glad to help me with the work, but they're getting on in years. Mother wrote that she's tired of standing all day long and Father wants Mother to rest. We could live upstairs over the bakery, where they live now. It's quite cozy, you know, and the heat from the ovens lingers upstairs so that it stays warm. Smells rather good, too," he told her, his eyes alight with the memory.

"But where on earth would they go? Your parents?" Katherine was accustomed to somewhat crowded living conditions, but an upstairs flat over a bakery could not be expected to comfortably house two married couples and two young children.

He smiled fondly. "Father has a hankering to return to Ireland. He met Mother there, you know. Even though he's English, he thought Ireland the loveliest place he'd ever seen. They want to go there."

Katherine stared at Peter as if he were spinning a children's story. "But Peter," she said, "I thought they needed your wages and that's why you're working here."

"So it is," he nodded. "But Father paid off the loan for the new ovens and he doesn't owe that money anymore. So what do you say? Do you think you could be a baker's wife?"

A baker's wife. Working with Peter and sharing his life in a bakery. She knew how to bake bread, what woman did not? Making sweet things to eat that people relished, would that not be a pleasant way to earn one's living? Having living quarters overhead that were clean, and warm, with no cracks in the windows or dampness in the walls. It didn't sound as if it could possibly be something that Katherine could expect in her life.

"Your parents," she said suddenly. "They may not approve. They may not want you to marry a woman who already has two children."

Peter laughed out loud. "They know your children, Katherine. The women in your neighbourhood send your son to the bakery to buy their bread and cakes. Sometimes they give him a penny for his work and he spends it on treats for himself and Rose. Mother is always saying what well-behaved children they are."

It was good to hear praise of her children. Still, they would need to meet Peter. She couldn't promise anything to anyone until she was certain that the four of them could become a family.

"What are you thinking?" Peter asked, watching as her conflicting emotions played across her face.

"What if we're hoping for something that we can't have, Peter?"

Peter studied her, his expression calm. "Why shouldn't we have what we want?" he asked logically.

Katherine's shoulders, which had tightened with the conviction that matters would not go as she hoped, immediately relaxed. "Oh, Peter," she exclaimed, "you make the impossible seem as if it's what I should expect."

Peter put his finger beneath her chin and tilted her face up. "Perhaps you see things as impossible when all they need is a bit of adjusting," he suggested with a mischievous grin. "With God and a willingness to try, what seems impossible at first might just work out quite well."

A HARD GOODBYE

Peter's words lit up a flicker of hope within her that perhaps he was right and life, so demanding for so long, might offer more than unceasing dread for what tomorrow might bring. Nonetheless, she could not help but be apprehensive when the train reached its destination in Birmingham and Katherine left the platform to make her way to the Murphy lodgings.

They did not know she was coming, neither the children nor Gerry. She had settled into her room at the Widow Makepeace's boarding house. The Widow Makepeace was, as Peter had said, a kind woman who had welcomed Katherine as a tenant. She was also earning wages by helping the landlady with the laundry and the cooking. Adjusting to London would be enough of a transition for the children as they would get to know Peter. Katherine realized that she, too, would be getting to know Peter in the role of a future husband. She hoped that everything would work out for the best.

Mrs Murphy answered her knock. Her eyes widened when she saw Katherine standing at the door. "Saints alive, lass!" she cried out. "'Tis good to see you, but you never sent word that you were coming or I'd have made more for supper than just soup."

"Mama!" Rose, hearing her mother's voice, burst from the kitchen, her braided hair flying behind her as she ran to her mother's arms. The pallor was gone from her face and her eyes were sparkling.

Katherine swept her daughter up in her arms. "Don't you look all bright and healthy now."

"She runs and plays with nary a cough," Mrs Murphy said, crossing over to the fireplace to stir the soup bubbling in the kettle. "Seamus will be along soon; he's just run to the bakery for an extra loaf of bread. The Edgewoods sell their bread at half-price at the end of the day," she explained to Katherine. "'Tis very good bread and at such a price, it's quite the bargain."

"The Edgewoods," Katherine stammered, caught off guard at hearing that name which was so much in her thoughts.

"To be sure," Mrs Murphy said. "I do hear that they want Peter to come back to Birmingham to run the bakery. Gerry will be home soon; he told you that he's leaving for America?" Mrs Murphy shook her head. "I suppose it's for the best. He says there's no future for the Irish here." She gave Katherine a sidelong glance. "I'd always hoped... "

Katherine was relieved that Seamus came in just at that moment, a loaf of bread under his arm. When he saw his mother standing in the kitchen, he promptly let go of the bread and only Katherine's quick action kept it from falling to the floor.

"Mama, what are you doing here?" he asked after he'd squeezed his mother around the waist in a strenuous embrace.

"I—Gerry's letter told me that he's leaving for America," Katherine said, struggling with the words. "I came to fetch you."

Mrs Murphy stood over the soup pot, the ladle raised. "You're taking the children?" she said in disbelief.

"I—I can't leave them here," Katherine returned awkwardly. "You'll all be planning your voyage."

"Yes, but, they're like me own now," Mrs Murphy said and to Katherine's dismay, she burst into tears. Rose and Seamus, confused by the reaction, raised their voices above Mrs Murphy's wailing to ask where Katherine was going to take them.

It was into this scene that Gerry, followed by his brother Eamon, entered the flat. An expression of hope transformed Gerry's face for just a moment until he saw her expression and heard his mother's tears.

"You're not going to America with us," he said flatly as he took off his coat and cap.

"No, I . . . " she faltered. "I don't think. . . "

"She's taking the children!" Mrs Murphy sobbed.

Gerry turned to Katherine. "You're taking the children away?"

"They can't stay here," she answered. "Not with you leaving."

"But—"

It was clear that Gerry had not come to this conclusion when making his plans. He had, Katherine guessed, assumed that she would go with him and the children as well. Rose began to cry and Seamus looked up at his mother with trepidation. Katherine realized that the Murphys had done such a superior job of looking after her children that, after the past few months, the two Foleys had been absorbed into the Murphy family.

"You're making a mistake," Gerry said. "They're happy with us"

Eamon, a quiet lad who didn't like discord, mumbled something and went back outside, preferring the cold weather to the rising temperature within the flat.

"You've been very good to them and I'm grateful," Katherine said, doing her best to keep her voice level while the chaotic emotions spun around her. "I don't want to live in America."

"You want to live in London?" Gerry replied incredulously. "London! You'll take them to London! Are you turning English?" The room, illuminated by the fireplace and candles, created shadows that cast their outlines upon Gerry's features, making him look like a stranger to Katherine.

Katherine, with an effort, ignored that remark. "I'll come back to Birmingham one day," she said. She could not announce that she would return to Birmingham as the wife of Peter Edgewood, the baker's son. That would have made the already volatile situation even more so. "You'll be in Boston."

"Not all at once, we won't. Gerry is going to go over first," Mrs Murphy explained. "Then send for us when he's saved up the fare."

"Where are the girls?" Katherine asked, eager for any distraction that would change the thrust of the topic.

"Alanna is minding the Houlihan's baby now that the missus has to work. Her Patrick fell ill of fever and died," Mrs Murphy told her. "I've sent you a letter, but you must not have gotten it yet. Maire, she's visiting Kathleen Hearne, but if she thinks I don't know that it's really that scamp Aidan Hearne she's there to see, then she doesn't know her Ma very well. I declare that I'll be sending her off to American with Gerry first, just to keep her out of trouble."

Gerry was unusually silent, standing in the room, his eyes fixed upon her as if he didn't recognize her. Rose and Seamus were clinging to Katherine, Rose crying, Seamus silent with the weight of what he didn't understand robbing him of words.

Katherine thought back to what Peter had said: *"With God and a willingness to try, what seems impossible at first might just work out quite well."* She wished he was here now to sort out the tangled knot of hurt and tears that she had unintentionally woven by her arrival. How could she fix this so that peace was restored? This was a family she loved, a family that had stood by her from the moment she arrived in Birmingham as an impoverished widow with two children desperate to make a new life for her family, another refugee from the Great Famine. It would be so easy to join them. She could marry Gerry and know that he would be a good father to her children. There was nothing new to learn, no uncharted territory of emotions to navigate. It would be so much easier.

Gerry, seeing the indecision on her face, pressed his point. "Marry me, Katherine," he said impulsively "Rose and Seamus are already part of the family. Let's make it official!"

"I'm going to marry someone else," she said. It was not what she intended to say. But the words sprang forth from her lips of their own volition, propelled by the knowledge that she did not love Gerry. She was fond of him and he was a good friend, and she was grateful for all that he had done. But that was not enough for marriage.

The room grew quiet. Mrs Murphy, the soup ladle in hand, stood frozen as if she could not believe what she had heard. Gerry stared as well, but his eyes were anything but frozen. They were molten with anger. "What if Rose and Seamus don't like him?" he challenged her, his outstretched arms gesturing toward the children clutching at her dress. "What if you're making a terrible mistake, one that will ruin your family, all for some foolish impulse that you've confused for lasting affection?"

"I must trust God," Katherine said.

"You're selfish, thinking only of yourself, not what's best for them." Gerry charged, raking his fingers through his hair as if he wanted to pull it out. He bent down before the children, his arms reaching out. "Tell the truth, Rose and Seamus, where would you rather be? Here or in London?"

"Gerry, don't do this," Katherine pleaded. She could feel the trembling in her children as they were confronted with this momentous decision.

"We want to be with Mama," Seamus said at last.

Gerry stood. "You're putting your children in an impossible situation!"

Peter's words, now planted within her, came forth. "With God and a willingness to try, what seems impossible at first might just work out quite well."

"Then you'd best leave now," Gerry said stiffly. 'You've made your feelings quite clear."

"Gerry!" his mother protested.

But Gerry turned away.

By the time Katherine, with Mrs Murphy's weeping assistance, had packed her children's belongings and taken them to say goodbye to the Murphy girls, it was time to go to the train station. As they departed the Murphy flat with hugs and tears, Gerry emerged from the shadows.

Without a word, he took the carpetbag from her hands. "I'll walk you to the station," he said.

"Gerry, I'm so sorry," Katherine told him. "I never wanted to hurt you. I'm grateful to you—"

"Could you please," Gerry said through clenched teeth, "leave off talking about gratitude. I've done a lot of thinking, thinking that I ought to have done before this. What was gratitude from you, I took to be something more. I want you to be happy. I want Rose and Seamus to be happy."

"I want you to be happy, Gerry," Katherine said honestly. The children walked at her side, holding her hand. They were silent, but Katherine knew that they, too, had made their choice. They were going to trust her that what seemed impossible was the path that God had chosen for their family. "You'll—I hope you'll write when you get to America? I want to know how you're faring. We'll always be friends, if you'll let it be so."

"Aye," Gerry said. "Maybe one day, that won't sound to me like bare toast without any jam to sweeten the taste," he told her, trying to smile. "You'll send me your new address?"

They had reached the train station. Seamus and Rose gaped in amazement as the majestic train pulled into the station, its imposing size and noise inspiring wonder.

"If you send it to the Edgewood Bakery," Katherine said, hating to hurt Gerry with this one final thrust, but knowing that the truth must be told, "it'll come to me."

Gerry stared. Swallowed. Walked woodenly beside her to the station platform.

"Peter's a good man," he said finally. He bent down to the children and enfolded them in a hug. "I'll expect letters from you two," he said, his tone undeniably fond and free of the tensions that shackled his words to Katherine.

"Plenty of letters. Just because I'll be in America doesn't mean I'll forget you. You mind me, now."

"They'll write," Katherine promised. "They'll want to know how you're faring."

Gerry rose. "Goodbye, Katie," he said. He kissed her on the cheek and, without another word, turned away.

Katherine looked back once, but the smoke from the train had created a diaphanous wall throughout the train station and she could not see him clearly.

"Come, children, it's time to board," Katherine told them. She remembered how uncertain she had been on that first train ride to London. Peter had been there to help her. The thought that with this train ride, she was returning to the promise of the new love she had found gave her confidence. God, she realized, had been the train conductor all along!

THE BAKERY IN BIRMINGHAM

"Are you sure I don't have flour in my hair?" Katherine turned around slowly so that her mother-in-law could inspect her.

Mrs Edgewood looked carefully at her daughter-in-law. "You're as pretty as always, my dear," she answered, surveying the young woman before her. Impulsively, for she was not a demonstrative woman, Mrs Edgewood gave Katherine a hug. "Peter is such a lucky man."

Katherine's striped green dress with its white collar and cuffs was more fashionable than anything she'd ever worn, but Peter was firm. She had earned the dress, he said, and more. With Katherine's energy and pleasant manner, along with her own baking skills, the bakery was busier than ever, so much so that the young couple was already saving money up so that they could buy the building from the man who rented it to them.

Peter came into the parlour then, looking quite stylish himself in his black waistcoat and trousers and white shirt. His brown locks were as unmanageable as ever, but to Katherine, they added to his charm, lending a spontaneity to his composed manner. "Turn around again," he directed. "I want to see for myself how lovely you look. "And," he added as his lips brushed against hers, "to steal a kiss."

"Who's this lovely woman in our midst?" Aloysius Edgewood wanted to know as he came up the stairs from the bakery in a waft of sugary air, Rose and Seamus each holding one of his hands.

"It's Mama, Grandad," Rose told him, her upturned face smiling at the big man in the white apron at her side.

"Why, so it is," her grandfather nodded. "Now, you all stand by your mother. You too, Peter. Let Mother and me take a good look at you."

Peter had insisted that Katherine was to have a new dress for today, and the children, too, were to have new clothes and shoes. They had to look their best, he had explained, because they were going to see the Crystal Palace, the Great Exhibition that he and their mother had helped to build.

Peter went to stand at her side, tall and proud, his hands resting upon the shoulders of Seamus, who stood in front of him, wearing a new waistcoat as well. Rose took her place in front of her mother, her own pink dress contrasting against the background of her mother's frock. They had stood in these positions in the early spring when they had gotten their photographs taken on the day that Katherine and Peter were married by Father Cleary.

The Edgewoods had not left for Ireland yet, but had already bought their little cottage and would soon be departing for their new home. Today, they would manage the bakery on their own, as they had done before Peter returned to Birmingham with his new family, while Peter, Katherine and the children went to London.

The older Edgewoods smiled at the sight before them. Then Mrs Edgewood, mindful of the time, clapped her hands. "Off with you now, or you'll miss the train!"

"Do you still prefer a donkey cart to train travel?" Peter teased once the train started on its way.

He had purchased tickets in the second-class section so that the trip, although not as posh as first-class travel, would be an improvement over third-class seats.

He put his hand over hers, one of the many small ways in which Peter displayed his affections. Katherine smiled at him. "When I'm with you and the children, I don't mind how we get to where we're going as long as we're together."

She leaned her head against Peter's shoulder. In the seats across from her, Seamus and Rose were chattering excitedly, no longer novices at the form of travel that had been so alarming to Katherine when she was first introduced to it only the year before.

How much had changed in the months since she'd journeyed to London, not knowing that the Birmingham baker's son who had travelled with her was the man God intended for her to marry.

"We'll be visiting Ireland at times, too," Peter reminded her.

"Yes, but that will be by boat. I don't mind that."

It would be nice to visit Ireland again, Katherine thought. The children would be able to see the beautiful land in which they were born. Living above the bakery was very different from the neighbourhood they'd been familiar with in the Birmingham slum where Katherine had lived upon her arrival in England. Now, they lived and worked among other shopkeepers and tradesmen in neat, trim businesses with living quarters above. In distance, it was not far from her former home, but in truth, it was worlds away.

The thought of distance brought to mind the letter she had received yesterday from America. She had been so busy preparing for today that she hadn't had a chance to read it. Remembering it now, she pulled it from her reticule.

"It's from Gerry," she told Peter as she opened the letter. "It came yesterday. Children, there's a letter from America from Gerry."

The children stopped their chatter to listen.

Dear Katie, she read aloud, keeping her voice low to avoid disturbing other passengers, but loud enough to be heard over the noise of the train, *I hope this letter finds you well. I'll be sending home the fare for Ma and the others to join me here in Boston. It's a grand city. The Beacon Hill toffs don't like us Irish much, but there are so many of us that they'll have to accept us one day! I'm working in a livery stable, can you believe it? It's a marvellous thing to be around horses again, something I never thought would happen.*

I've found lodgings, too, in the Irish section. It's noisy and crowded and it reminds me of our neighbourhood in Birmingham. There's room for the family when they arrive.

Katherine interrupted herself. "We must go and visit Mrs Murphy before they all leave," she said to the children.

"Can we bring them a cake?" Seamus wanted to know. "Eamon always liked the cakes from the bakery."

"You may bring them a little cake for each one of the family," Peter said in amusement. "You can help me bake them."

Katherine continued reading the letter. *I've met a lovely girl. Her name is* Althne *, just like my sister. Her father owns the livery stable and he says that when we're married, he'll* *make me a partner in the business. Can you believe it? You'd like* Althne *; she's cheerful and always has a smile for everyone. She loves horses too, and we go riding every day.*

Katie, I want to tell you how thankful I am that you followed your heart when you said you couldn't marry me. You said that God can make the impossible happen. I didn't believe you then, but it turns out you were right. I believe that Althne *and I will be happy together and I'm sure that she'll fit right in with us Murphys.*

Give my love to the children, and I hope that they're happy with Peter as their father. I hope that you're happy as well. Our roads have travelled very different paths, but you were right all along. We're friends and that's a very good thing.

Gerry

The children listened as Katherine read the letter but when she finished, they returned to their perusal of the scenery outside the train window. Katherine realized that for them, Gerry was part of the past. They remembered him, but they too were living new lives now, as he was.

"He sounds as if he's happy," Peter commented after Katherine folded the letter and put it away.

"I hope so. He's a good man."

She lifted her head to see Peter's warm brown eyes smiling down upon her. With Peter, there was no need to explain the nuances that had so troubled her when she was making her decisions. He already knew and understood. And even when his lips weren't touching hers, there was always a kiss in his eyes.

"There it is!"

The children stopped walking and stared at the massive edifice that was the Crystal Palace. In the sunshine of the June day, the light glittered off the glass walls of the building, as if the panels had been gilded in gold. Crowds were streaming toward the Crystal Palace, eager to see the displays inside and take part in this magnificent exhibition of the prowess and innovation of the British Empire.

"You and Mama built this?" Seamus exclaimed in awe.

"Not by ourselves," Peter said as he lifted Rose up in his arms so that she could see over the throng. "We had lots of others along with us. Your mother was in charge of the plants."

"And the elm trees," Katherine added.

"What did you do, Papa?" Rose wanted to know.

"I helped to build the walls that you see now. It looked very different then, didn't it, Katherine?"

So many scenes flashed before Katherine's eyes. Mick Killian on the floor after the accident that took his arm.

The snow falling on Peter's cap when she went to tell him goodbye, little knowing that she'd be back the same day because she had learned that she loved him. Other scenes, too, but the unpleasant ones could be pushed aside. They were memories, but they no longer mattered. Mr. Brown's illicit interest, Blanche's morbid delight in sharing the bad news of the Crystal Palace accident, they belonged to another Katherine.

Katherine Foley had been a fearful woman, waiting for the ill-intentioned fate to strike. Katherine Edgewood knew that by trusting in God and having a willingness to try, what seemed impossible at first had worked out quite well.

Excitement welled up inside her and an eagerness to see the final result of those months of hard work and separation from her family. They had brought Rose to health, and they had brought them all to Peter.

"Let's go inside," she urged them. "I want us to see everything!"

THANK YOU FOR CHOOSING A PUREREAD BOOK!

We hope you enjoyed the story, and as a way to thank you for choosing PureRead we'd like to send you this free book, and other fun reader rewards…

Click here for your free copy of Whitechapel Waif
PureRead.com/victorian

Thanks again for reading.
See you soon!

IF YOU LOVED SLUM MOTHER'S SACRIFICE...

Continue reading with another PureRead tale of romance and resilience.

For your enjoyment here is the first chapter of The Manchester Maid by Rosie Swan.

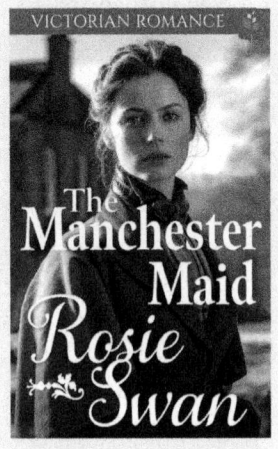

The dream

The Irish Sea

1840

It was the third night in a row that Harvey Matthews dreamed of home. Every night the dream was the same. His dear wife Hazel would come to him while holding a precious bundle wrapped up in a colourful baby blanket. "Harvey," she would say, hardly able to contain her joy, "Look what God gave us." She would then pull aside part of the blanket, so he could have a good look at the package in her slender arms.

And as Harvey looked, his eyes widened.

There, safely tucked away against Hazel's chest, was the pink scalp of a new-born babe with a tiny tuft of auburn colored hair sticking out right in the middle. It was a sight so precious, so pure and fresh.

A child? Was that baby his? He had not known Hazel was pregnant.

"Is it… mine?" Even in his dream, he knew it was an offensive question, but he had to know. When had all this happened?

Hazel however, wasn't disturbed by his attitude. Her joy was too great to be spoiled by Harvey's sceptical approach. She was just radiant and carried a beauty that Harvey had rarely seen in his life. While he dearly loved his wife, it was common knowledge she could not be classified among the prettiest of women in town, at least not by the worldly standards most men adhered to. But now, in his dream, it seemed an angel from heaven had dipped his celestial paintbrush in some sort of heavenly veneer and had not been stingy in applying the glorious elixir to his wife. She no longer resembled the somewhat slovenly woman with her tense lips and nervously darting eyes that he was so used to. The look of tension and difficulty that would tell him she worried about a thousand-and-one things, problems she should never be worried about but that made him feel like a poor fisherman from Blackpool, and a stumbling husband who could never do right.

But not in the dreams.

In the dreams she had not just been *touched* by an angel, rather she *appeared* as one. Instead of answering Harvey's rude question in a way that he would have deserved by saying something like, "Are you suggesting I've been unfaithful to you, Harvey Matthews? Shame on you," she gave him the sweetest smile and whispered, "Yes, love… this child is yours. This is God's blessing."

And every night he dreamed this part, his reaction was the same. It was a feeling of joy, unbridled joy. The baby was *his*. Truly his. Upon hearing Hazel's gentle reassurance, he allowed her happiness to spread to his own heart. "A baby… I am a father now." As he stared in awe at the tender miracle before him, he realized this was a sacred moment. This was one of those rare instances where heaven touched the dreary world of the common life. The veil between this life of toil and suffering and the unseen realm of perfection had been pulled away, and he was allowed a rare peek into eternity. That baby came from a sphere of perfection where everything made sense and where sin, poverty and evil could not molest.

And in the dream it was a girl, every time. How could dreams be so similar? Hazel would show her to him. She would pull back a bit more of the blanket so Harvey could have a better look. Wonderful... The child stared at him with large green eyes while sucking on one of her tiny fingers, and looked at him as if he were the best man in the world.

A girl... He had been given a girl. If it had been a choice, Harvey would have opted for a boy. Boys could bring in more money, but right now he was too excited to think about that. Who was he anyway, to complain about such a wonderful blessing?

But then the dream would take a turn for the worse. It happened every night. Right when he held out his hands, expecting Hazel to hand him the babe, he was pulled back by an unseen force; terrible and dark. A gale had come out of nowhere, a wind so strong that there was nothing he could do to fight it. A scream erupted from his throat and he began to wave his arms around in a futile effort to stand his ground, but he never succeeded. He was powerless and faster and faster he was being pulled into a dark pool of nothingness.

He could still see Hazel's face from a distance. It no longer carried the heavenly expression of grateful joy but had turned into a desperate grimace of helplessness and fear. "Harvey!" she cried out. "Don't leave me!" It was a despondent wail, so loud and clear that it shattered Harvey's heart. He wanted to tell her he loved her, but he could not. No words would come out of his mouth and a sickening reality dawned on him that maybe he was just about to... die. But he *could* not die. He had a wife and a baby to take care of.

At that point Harvey would wake up from the dream; three times in a row now.

It had been the exact same thing every night. He woke up, confused and bewildered, his heart pounding and the images of the dream still sharply etched on his conscious perception. Again that dream...

For just a brief moment he did not know where he was, but then, as the sound of creaking wood entered his ears and he felt the swaying and the rocking of the boat, he remembered again. He was still sailing on The Bullfrog, somewhere out in the middle of the Irish Sea, and he and the others were on their way home after a successful fishing trip. The days had been sunny, and the nights still. Perfect for fishing, but now the wind had increased in strength. He could feel it by the force with which their little vessel was being tossed up and down on the waves. Judging by the force with which the vessel shook and creaked, he realized they needed him on deck. Recently, he had become the First Mate, which meant he worked right under Master Farren and was qualified to handle the boat in rough weather.

Still, that dream... it troubled him. Why did he have this same dream, three nights in a row? It always started so wonderful, almost heavenly, but then it would end like a regular nightmare. He could not shake off the memory of the look of panic on Hazel's face and could still hear her screams, even now, as he sat up straight on the straw ticking on which he had been lying.

But then, this was only a dream. Dreams were not to be trusted. Dreams were no signs or guides for the way one was to live his own life. Most likely, as Master Farren claimed, dreams were caused by a mixture of your heart's unfulfilled desires, worries about life, and the overload of tea, fish and more fish, so annoyingly present while out at sea for five days in a row. That was probably true. Last night, he had just eaten too much treacle with his potatoes.

Nevertheless, true or not true, Harvey was shook up. He rubbed his eyes and shook his head in a futile effort to shake off his visions of the night. The others needed him. What time was it anyway? He looked up and squinted his eyes as he scanned the room. Above him, in the ceiling and right around the hatch that led to the deck, was a small trickle of light that seeped through the cracks, signifying the new day had made its appearance. Only one more day of sailing and they would be home in Blackpool.

The desire to take Hazel in his arms and pull her close to his chest became almost overwhelming. He was not a man that was easily given over to unstable emotions and fickle feelings. He was better than those foolish people who fell apart at the least bit of trouble and would whine like a baby. But after having had these disturbing dreams, he desperately wanted to see Hazel again and hold her and take care of her.

Tomorrow. Then he would ask her straight out if she was with child and after they had had a good laugh about his silly behaviour and she would have chided him for having these weird dreams, he would close the curtains of the bedroom in their small rented place in Gloucester Street and kiss her. Yes, that was what he would do… Tomorrow, after they had disembarked in the harbour and he had helped to transport the fish they had caught, he would see Hazel and everything would be all right.

He threw off the coarse blanket that had kept him warm throughout the night, got up and made his way to the wooden steps that led up to the deck.

When he opened the hatch and stuck out his head, he was welcomed by a cold, harsh wind filled with heavy raindrops that gushed down his face. Corwine Musselwhite, the third mate, was just passing by and cast him a wide grin. "Right on time, sir. I hadn't counted on rain," he exclaimed. "I was just going to get you. Farren wants you."

Harvey climbed out all the way and walked over to the railing with difficulty. Wherever he looked legions of dark clouds, like angry horsemen from an invading enemy, swept over the foamy wild sea.

Normally, Harvey loved such weather. It was always a fight to steer their boat right through the storm into the safety of the Blackpool harbour. A fight with the elements, but a fight he and his buddies would always win.

But today Harvey wasn't so sure of himself. The dark pull toward death in his dream had been so real, and Hazel's face had been so terrified...

Master Farren was standing near the back of the boat, holding the wheel, and was impatiently motioning for him to take over. No doubt the Master had been sailing for hours on end while he had been sleeping... and dreaming.

Just then the boat went down again in a valley of water, surrounded by massive walls of salty foam. As Harvey made his way forward, he held on tight. This was no ordinary storm and it was fast getting worse. Right above his head, he heard the desperate shriek of a seagull. He spotted the little fellow and stared at it in amazement. Seagulls, so far out at sea, and always hoping for a handout and an easy dinner. But there would be no handout today, and it appeared the struggle against the gale was getting too much for the little fellow. The bird simply landed on the bobbing, furious waves as if he was sitting in an easy chair. A grim smile appeared around Harvey's mouth. Smart bird. If you can't beat it, just join it. But for him and the crew, it would not be so easy.

"It's going to be quite a storm, Harvey," Master Farren cried out above the wind when Harvey had reached him. "But nothing you and I cannot handle."

"Of course, Skipper," Harvey replied. He admired the older fellow with his bushy beard and large, unkempt wild brows and deep-seated eyes. He had never seen the old tar afraid in all the years he had been working under him. First as a boy and a deckhand, then as fourth mate, third mate, and now, a few months ago, Master Farren had promoted him to First Mate. A wonderful change it was, as it meant better pay and more responsibility.

"Not afraid, are you?" Farren asked without looking at Harvey. Harvey couldn't help but grin. He wasn't afraid, but even if he was, Farren would be the last person he would show it to. "Of course not," he answered indignantly. "You want me to take over?"

The seasoned sailor nodded. "Just for a while. Nature is calling, but I'll be back. This is going to be a serious challenge. It's getting worse, you know. Have you seen it?"

"Seen what?"

"There," Farren took one of his hands off the wheel and pointed in the direction from where Harvey had come. "Look south."

Harvey turned in the direction Farren was pointing and swallowed hard.

The clouds that were rolling in from there were darker than any he had ever seen at sea, and they were spreading fast. Even though it was still morning, they would soon be plunged into total darkness.

"Take the wheel," Farren ordered in a loud voice. "I'll be back in a minute."

Harvey grabbed the wheel as Farren walked off. Afraid? Afraid of a minor storm…? Of course not. He was worth his salt. But true, this was going to be a storm unlike all the others he had experienced.

Earlier, Farren had already given the orders to lower the mainsail and raise the smaller storm sail that would help them manoeuvre more speedily. Cormine Musselwhite and Tate Hample, the fourth mate, were struggling to do as they were told. The work was progressing slowly, because of the violent shaking and bobbing. Too slow to Harvey's liking. If these two sailors didn't hurry, the mainsail could rip. "Hurry up with these sails," he yelled from a distance, knowing full well his statement would not make any difference as they could not even hear his voice over the roaring wind.

But then, right at a crucial moment, Cormine slipped on the rain-soaked deck. The sail came crashing down. The unfortunate man was still holding on to one of the ropes with both of his hands, but as a monstrous, surging wave washed over the deck and pushed the boat precariously to its side, the sailor disappearing from sight. A second later, a bright flash of lightning, much closer than Harvey liked, illuminated the raging waves around, and Harvey saw Cormine struggling to stay aboard. To Harvey's relief he saw how he crawled back to safety. The lightning flash was instantly followed by the terrifying roar of a thunderclap, so close and so loud that Harvey feared the ship had been hit and had snapped in twain.

"Come on," Harvey shouted into the wind, wanting to encourage himself. "I am not afraid of you. Is that all you got?"

But he knew this was no regular storm. It appeared the mouth of hell had opened and all its ugly demons had been unleashed and were now letting down their fury on the helpless vessel. Harvey held on to the wheel with all of his might, gritting his teeth, barely able to think. It was all he could do to keep from being swung overboard as the ship tilted down again to the side and Harvey saw how the foamy, dark green waters now almost reached his boots. Then, with a violent shake, the ship was pushed back up again. Dear God, have mercy...

Sail right into the storm... right into the storm, Harvey mumbled as he kept following the procedures he had learned from Farren, but it was so difficult to keep the ship steady.

"Let me have the wheel," a voice shouted in his ears. Farren was back. "Right into the waves, Harvey."

Right when he was about to step aside to hand the wheel back to Farren an unexpected wave threw Harvey off and the wheel slipped out of his hands. Instantly the helpless boat tipped precariously to its side.

Harvey had nothing to hold on to anymore, and lost his balance. As the ship tilted very far starboard he slipped and let out a guttural roar, swinging his arms around in hopes of finding something to hold onto. But he did not. Seconds later he plunged into the foaming sea.

Instantly the cold salty water was all around. He yelled for help but all he got was waves that smashed into his face, filling his lungs with salty water. They felt like they were about to burst... He needed air, but there was no air. There was only water, cold, dark and foul. Where was the surface? He could not be very far from the surface, but he could not find it.

He wanted air, but all he got was water. At that point, he understood he was going to die... He would never see dear Hazel again. His dream had been real. He was now being pulled away by the darkness, just like he had been in his dream. Hazel would be desperate. Without him, she could not take care of her own life anymore. The poorhouse was the only place she could go to. And a child... she was with child...

God, please...

"Fear not. I am with you always."

What? Who was talking?

It was the strangest experience, but despite being in the depths of the belly of the sea where nobody could talk, Harvey heard a distinct voice. It was as loud and clear as he had heard Master Farren say only moments earlier that he wanted to take over the wheel. But this voice was calm, almost tender, and spoken with the utmost of grace.

"Today, you will be with me in Paradise," the voice continued.

Paradise?

Where had he heard those words again? Then he knew. The Saviour had spoken these words to the thief who had been hanging on a cross next to him. The Saviour was here, right next to him in the water. He was with him even during his last desperate moments on earth.

So all would be well then. There was no reason to be afraid.

After these words Harvey no longer struggled, but somehow allowed himself to just float through the troubled waters and, strangely enough, a deep, unearthly peace settled on his heart.

"You will have a daughter upon earth and she will be called Alice, for she will be noble and kind," the voice continued.

A daughter? But he would never see her, as he was going to die. It didn't matter for somehow, all would be well. The Saviour had told him so. And that was enough for Harvey.

Then his heart stopped beating…

Continue Reading The Manchester Maid on Amazon

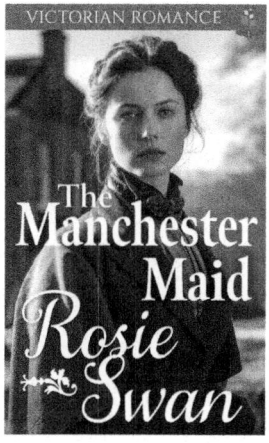

LOVE VICTORIAN ROMANCE?

If you enjoyed this story why not continue straight away with other books in our PureRead Victorian Romance library?

Read them all...

Victorian Slum Girl's Dream

Poor Girl's Hope

The Lost Orphan of Cheapside

Born a Workhouse Baby

The Lowly Maid's Triumph

Poor Girl's Hope

The Victorian Millhouse Sisters

Dora's Workhouse Child

Saltwick River Orphan

Workhouse Girl and The Veiled Lady

OUR GIFT TO YOU

AS A WAY TO SAY THANK YOU WE WOULD LOVE TO SEND YOU THIS BEAUTIFUL STORY FREE OF CHARGE.

Click here for your free copy of Whitechapel Waif

PureRead.com/victorian

At PureRead we publish books you can trust. Great tales without smut or swearing, but with all of the mystery and romance you expect from a great story.

Be the first to know when we release new books, take part in our fun competitions, and get surprise free books in your inbox by signing up to our free VIP Reader list.

As a welcome gift you'll receive the story of the Whitechapel Waif straight to your inbox...

Click here for your free copy of Whitechapel Waif

PureRead.com/victorian

Printed in Great Britain
by Amazon